"You're lady!" Sean laughed

"I've no more idea what's going on in that mixed-up mind of yours than if you were one of those damned fish."

"Maybe I just don't like the bait you're offering," she jibed.

"Maybe you just haven't tasted enough of it yet." He caught her quickly, and his kiss was an invasion that ravaged her mouth with its fierce demand. His powerful hands held her curved intimately against his hard body, reminding her of the danger she'd so recklessly courted. Her own body responded treacherously, and sensing her defeat, he thrust her away.

"Let that be a lesson to you," he warned roughly. "Don't start anything you haven't the guts to finish."

"Don't ever touch me again," she snapped at him. "I'll kill you."

"Don't tempt me, little Kate," he taunted. "That sure would be one hell of a way to go!"

SUSANNE McCARTHY has spent most of her life in London, but after her marriage she and her husband moved to Shropshire, and the author is now an enthusiastic advocate of this unspoiled part of England. So although her first romance novel, *A Long Way From Heaven*, was set in the sunny Caribbean, Suzanne says that the English countryside may feature in her future writing.

Books by Susanne McCarthy

SUSANNE McCARTHY

don't ask for tomorrow

Harlequin Books

TORONTO • NEW YORK • LONDON
AMSTERDAM • PARIS • SYDNEY • HAMBURG
STOCKHOLM • ATHENS • TOKYO • MILAN

Harlequin Presents first edition December 1987
ISBN 0-373-11036-7

Original hardcover edition published in 1987
by Mills & Boon Limited

CHAPTER ONE

'I'M sorry, Mrs Taylor, but Mr Thompson isn't free.'

Kate drew herself up to her full height of five feet one inch. 'Please tell Mr Thompson that if he doesn't see me *now*, he can expect to hear from my solicitor on a libel suit.'

The secretary sighed, and touched the key of the intercom on her desk with one immaculately manicured fingertip. 'I'm very sorry to trouble you again, Mr Thompson, but Mrs Taylor is most insistent that she should see you at once. She's speaking of legal action.'

Kate heard an impatient sigh, and then Mr Thompson conceded with an air of resignation. 'Very well. Show her in.'

'Yes, Mr Thompson.' The secretary stood up, her face impassive. 'Please come this way.'

She led Kate through an inner door, into an imposing carpeted office. A grey-haired man sat behind a vast desk littered with papers, and he didn't even bother to look up as Kate walked in. Her anger exploded. She marched up to the desk, and slammed the magazine down on it, together with the old logbook.

He looked across at both articles and then up at Kate, surprised that she should dare to challenge him so assertively. 'What's this?' he asked, frowning.

'This,' stated Kate, pointing at the magazine, 'is your magazine, containing a libellous article about my husband. And this is the proof,' she added, tossing the log-book across the desk towards him.

He picked it up and opened it. 'But this is just an old diary,' he protested.

'It's a record. My husband kept them for every dive he made,' she informed him with dignity. She took the log-book back from him, and searched quickly through the pages. 'There,' she said, handing it back to him. 'Read that.'

'"Distribution of cannon conforms to known armoury of *Belle Étoile*",' he read. He turned a page. '"Iron anchor of French Design, *circa* 1700."' He glanced up at Kate again. 'Very interesting,' he agreed, 'but it doesn't prove anything.'

Her dark eyes kindled. 'What more proof do you want?' she demanded hotly.

He leaned back in his executive chair and regarded her thoughtfully. So this was the woman who'd finally caught Dave Taylor, he mused. He could see why. She was a dainty little thing, but her figure curved in all the right places. A halo of dark curls framed a fine-boned, almost ethereal face—but those big, beautiful dark eyes could pack a lethal punch. If he were twenty years younger . . .

He put down his pen decisively and smiled at her, waving his hand towards a chair. 'Sit down, Mrs Taylor,' he invited in a conciliatory tone. She perched on the edge of the seat, her head still tilted at a proud angle as she waited for him to speak. 'The *Belle Étoile* has been surrounded by controversy ever since she sank,' he began.

'You don't have to tell me that,' she returned promptly. 'My husband knew more about her than anyone.'

He nodded, lifting a placating hand. 'Yes, I'm aware of that,' he agreed. 'But though he claimed to have found the wreck once, he was never able to find her again, nor did he produce any conclusive proof.'

'You'd never have dared to publish that article if he were still alive to defend himself,' she challenged bitterly.

Mr Thompson shook his head. 'I'm sorry, Mrs Taylor. I had a great deal of respect for Dave, but the fact remains that the fate of the *Belle Étoile* is still not known.'

'You're accusing him of lying.'

'Now, I wouldn't . . .'

'Yes, you are,' she insisted forcefully. 'Well, I'll make you eat your words. I'll go out to the Bahamas myself, and find the wreck.'

Mr Thompson's eyebrows lifted in polite surprise. 'If you can do that, I'll be more than happy to print a retraction. I'll want photographs, of course—exclusively.'

Kate smiled confidently. 'I'll get them,' she asserted.

'Good.' He handed the log-book back to her. 'I wish you luck.'

Kate tucked the log-book into her leather shoulder-bag, and stood up. 'Thank you,' she said, a mischievous smile curving her mouth. 'There was just one more thing.'

'Such as?'

'Any chance of an advance?' she asked cheekily.

His lips twitched in an appreciative smile. 'You do have a cool nerve, Mrs Taylor,' he remarked, amused. 'Very well. I'll commission an article from you—our standard contract. See my secretary on your way out.'

The British Airways 747 banked and began its long, slow descent. Kate fastened her seat-belt, adjusted her watch to local time, and turned to gaze out of the window at the long chain of islands scattered in a magnificent sweep from Florida to the Caribbean.

The plane was too high up to allow her to see much detail of the land, but already she could feel the lure of the sparkling waters that lapped the shining white beaches—the warm, shallow Bahamian Sea, a tapestry in glorious Technicolor, every shade of the spectrum from clear, crystal green to a deep, majestic indigo.

Dave would have loved it. She glanced down at the gold wedding ring she still wore, and brushed a tear from the corner of her eye. He wouldn't want her to be crying. He had always been too busy getting on with his life to waste time looking back. 'Live for today,' he always used to say. 'Don't ask for tomorrow. If you spend all your life worrying about what might be round the next corner, you aren't really living at all.'

No one could ever have accused Dave Taylor of not living life to the full. Kate had first met him when, at eighteen, she had gone up to university. He used to stride around the stark concrete corridors of the life sciences building like some Viking warlord, his fiery red-gold hair ablaze. He lectured in marine biology, and his infectious enthusiasm for his subject had made him very popular with all the students.

He had also run the university's sub-aqua club, and it was there that Kate had enjoyed a much-envied advantage over all the other girls who had fancied him. She was already an experienced skin diver. Her mother was Greek, and every summer of her life had been spent at her grandparents' villa on the Gulf of Corinth. Her grandfather had taught her to dive as soon as she was old enough to wear a scuba suit.

At first she had been only one of a number of girls he

had flirted with, but gradually his interest in her had deepened. Their romance had blossomed on weekend field trips, diving in the interesting waters off Cornwall and southern Ireland, studying the fish and underwater plant life and indulging Dave's passion for exploring old wrecks.

But Kate had inherited from her mother not only her slightly exotic colouring, but also a rather old-fashioned attitude to the rules of love. She had always firmly refused to share a cabin with Dave aboard the old wooden fishing-boat the club had bought and renovated for their trips.

And then, one lunchtime just before Easter in her final year, he had suddenly announced, 'OK, you win! We'll get married!'

She had thought he must be joking, but he wasn't. With that usual bewildering impulsiveness he had dragged her off that very afternoon to make the arrangements, and they had been married two weeks later.

They had had just four months of idyllic happiness before he had been killed. It had been so cruel and sudden. He had been rigging some underwater lighting, and he had been electrocuted. Of course, there should have been circuit-breakers in use, but they'd found they were a couple short, and it had been too far to go back to harbour . . .

Could it really be almost a year ago? The time had passed so quickly. In those first few terrible weeks after Dave's death she had not wanted to go on living herself, had not thought it possible that she could. But slowly she had begun to emerge from that black despair, and as the months passed she had found that the pain was easing.

But then she had opened that magazine—one that

Dave had contributed to regularly—and her fragile peace of mind had been shattered. There was no way she could ignore it—she owed it to Dave to prove the truth of his claim beyond any further doubt.

Armed with all the information she could find, culled from Dave's detailed notes and every book that made any mention of the subject, she had her long summer vacation, the advance Mr Thompson had allowed her, and all her savings, and she was going to find the *Belle Étoile*.

Of course, it would be much easier if she could recruit the help of Sean McGregor, the skipper of the boat Dave had chartered on that first trip when he had found the wreck. A little determined detective work had uncovered the address of a man of that name who owned a boat called the *Barracuda*. She had written to him several weeks ago, outlining her plans and asking if the boat would be available for hire. Unfortunately he hadn't answered her letter yet.

She wondered vaguely what he was like. The name conjured up an image of a tough old sea-dog with grizzled hair and a pipe clenched firmly between his teeth. Why hadn't he written back? Maybe he couldn't write very well, she mused.

The plane touched down smoothly, and within a few minutes she was walking across the tarmac towards the airport building. The gentle, cooling breeze lifted her feathery dark curls and she had to put on her sunglasses against the brilliance of the morning sunlight. In spite of the lingering sadness of missing Dave, her spirits had begun to rise from the moment she had tasted that fresh, salt-tanged air.

The relaxed, friendly atmosphere of the islands had permeated even to the customs hall, making the tedious process of checking through all her bulky diving equipment and Dave's precious underwater camera far less irksome than she had anticipated.

It was an attractive drive into Nassau, skirting around the lovely shores of Lake Kilarney. She had booked into one of the cheaper hotels, and went straight up to her room, the effects of jet-lag making her sleepy.

But before she could rest she had an important phone call to make. The helpful operator got her the number, and after it had rung for quite a long time a woman's voice answered. 'Is Mr McGregor there please?' Kate asked politely.

'No, he ain't,' came the sharp response. 'Who is this?'

'My name is Kate Taylor—Mrs Kate Taylor,' she amended with emphasis. 'I wrote to Mr McGregor a few weeks ago, from England, about some business I want to discuss with him.'

'Oh ... yeah.' The young woman sounded slightly mollified. 'Well, he's gone fishing right now,' she conceded. 'I don't expect he'll be back till late. There was some sharks over by Spanish Wells.'

'Could you ask him to ring me, please?' Kate asked quickly. 'It is quite important.' She gave the phone number of the hotel, and then hung up. She was mildly intrigued, wondering who the woman was. Sean McGregor's wife? Or maybe his daughter? Somehow her image of him hadn't placed him in a domestic setting. With an idle shrug of her shoulders she dismissed the thought, and lay down on the bed to take a short nap before lunch.

She woke to find the room in darkness. She turned on the bedside light, and glancing at her watch in astonishment realised that she had slept for nearly eight hours. But now she felt refreshed and ready for anything. She checked with the hotel's switchboard, but Mr McGregor had not returned her call, so she asked the girl to try the number again.

A man answered the phone. 'Mr McGregor?' she asked hopefully.

'Who's speaking?' The voice was oddly evasive.

'It's Kate Taylor,' she answered. 'I rang earlier.'

'I'm sorry. Mr McGregor isn't here.'

Kate's eyes glinted with sharp suspicion. 'Do you know what time he'll be back?'

'Sorry, no.'

'I see.' She kept the irritation out of her voice. It was pointless getting annoyed with him. 'Well, thank you. I'll try again later.' She put the phone down, and glowered at it as if the instrument were to blame. Apparently Mr McGregor had sufficient employment to be able to turn away business. But at least he could have had the good manners to tell her so.

Or maybe he just didn't fancy the idea of taking a woman on a salvage expedition. There were dangers around these old wrecks, she was perfectly aware of that. She knew exactly what she was doing, of course, and would be taking no foolish risks. But she could well imagine that some of these local fishermen would be very superstitious.

She caught sight of herself in the mirror, and studied her reflection critically. She had lost weight since last year, and in spite of the honey-gold sheen of her skin she had an air of delicacy that had not been there before her marriage. It made her dark eyes look larger, her cheekbones more sculpted. She was not very tall, and for a moment she wondered if Mr McGregor might think her a little too fragile to undertake the rigours of a diving expedition. But since he hadn't even seen her, he was hardly in a position to judge. Well, dammit, he was going to find out that she was not so easily dismissed!

But at the moment all she could think about was getting something to eat. Kate unpacked her clothes quickly, and had a swift wash in the bathroom down the corridor. She put on a crushed cotton dress—one of only two she had brought with her—in a soft ice-pink that flattered her colouring. It tied across her shoulders with narrow straps and the skirt drifted round her knees. She wore high-heeled sandals and a little make-up to add a touch of sophistication, and was rewarded by several admiring glances as she took her seat in the dining-room.

The food was delicious. She tried a creamed conch chowder, and followed it with a sinfully fattening guava duff, drowned in rich rum sauce. The tangy Bahamian air had certainly lent an edge to her appetite! It was almost ten o'clock when she finished her meal, and in the hotel's bar a steel band was playing goombay music, a gentle, swaying sound, reminiscent of the lazy rhythm of the shallow Bahamian sea.

In the foyer she paused by the pay-phone, a frown creasing her brow. She was sure it had been Mr McGregor himself who had answered her call earlier in the evening. Ringing him again was not going to get her anywhere. She had to go and see him in person—at a time when he wouldn't be expecting her to show up.

She wasn't very keen to wander round a strange town at this time of night, but tonight might be her best chance of catching the elusive man off-guard. With an impatient shrug she dismissed her reservations and ran up to her room to fetch her jacket and a street-map of Nassau.

The capital of the Bahamas was pulsating with life, a glittering tinsel-world of bars and night-clubs. The air was still pleasantly warm, so she tossed her cream blazer over her arm as she threaded her way through the crowds of strollers. The sounds of goombay, calypso and jazz spilled from doorways all along Bay Street, mingling with the cheerful jangle of the harnesses of the ponies that drew the pretty surreys laden with tourists, and the frustrated grumbling of car engines held up in the heavy traffic.

She found the address easily enough—it was down near the waterfront. But as she approached it, her footsteps faltered. The doorway was rather unprepossessing: it was down a couple of steps, and above it a tawdry scarlet and gold neon sign flashed its message to the night—the Rum Runner. She glanced around, seeking another door, but there was none.

As she hesitated on the pavement, the door swung open and a couple of sailors lurched up the steps. She stepped back, but they saw her, and grinned at her drunkenly.

'Hello there, baby. What's up? Your boyfriend stood you up, has he? Why don't you come and have a little drinky with us, eh?' one of them invited, his voice slurred.

'No, thank you,' she responded as coolly as she could. 'I'm looking for someone.'

'Who are you looking for, honey?' the other one asked quite pleasantly. He seemed a little less drunk than his friend.

'Sean McGregor,' she told him. 'I understand he lives here.'

The first one leered at her. 'What's old Sean been up to, then? Got you into trouble, has he?'

Kate flushed scarlet with shock, but the more sober

one cuffed his friend into silence. 'Sure, he lives here,' he assured her. 'Come on, you don't want to go in there on your own.'

He stood aside for her politely, but still Kate hesitated. She didn't want to go in there at all. But she was determined to see Mr McGregor, and after all, what harm could come to her in the middle of Nassau? So, squaring her shoulders, she marched down the steps, the sailors on her heels.

Before she had gone five paces into the room she was regretting her recklessness. It was a dingy, smoke-filled cavern, noisy and crowded, and the few women present looked every bit as tough as the men. She felt as though scores of greedy eyes were burning into her, making her acutely aware of the feminine curves of her body beneath the delicate fabric of her dress. But it was too late to turn back. Instinctively she knew that she must not show fear.

The sailor took her arm and drew her towards the bar. 'Hey, Maxie!' he called cheerfully. 'Where's old Sean?'

A strikingly attractive blonde girl, in a dress cut low enough to start a riot, turned at his words. 'He's over there, with Sharps and Banadol, in a game of poker,' she told him as she served a customer with a foaming glass of beer.

Kate recognised the voice as the one that had answered the phone earlier in the day. 'I spoke to you this morning,' she said quickly. 'My name's Kate Taylor.'

'Oh, yeah!' The scarlet mouth curved into a wide and friendly smile. At a second glance, Kate could see that she wasn't quite as young as she had first appeared. She extended a beautifully manicured hand, and Kate shook it, slightly bemused. 'Hi. I'm

Maxie. I gave him your message. Didn't he ring you back? That's typical!' She raised her eyes expressively to the heavens. 'Well, it serves him right now that you've caught up with him. He's over there, playing cards.'

She pointed towards a group of half a dozen men, seated in intense concentration around a table littered with cards and money, oblivious of the noise and jostle around them. Kate thanked Maxie and the sailor with a friendly smile, and suppressing the nervous fluttering in the pit of her stomach, walked across to the table. One thing she *had* noticed: the mention of Sean McGregor's name had acted like a talisman on the leering customers. Many were still watching her with undisguised interest, but they seemed to have fallen back a pace.

The men around the card table, however, were completely ignoring her, and she had to raise her voice a little to make it heard. 'I'm looking for Sean McGregor,' she announced firmly.

There was a tense pause as the card players reluctantly acknowledged her intrusion and looked up at her. Slowly Kate became aware of one pair of cool blue eyes that were regarding her steadily. In the dim light she formed an impression of a hard-boned, weathered face not softened by the mocking smile that curved the rather ruthless mouth. Sun-bleached hair grew with wayward thickness, curling over a high, intelligent forehead, and there was a small, jagged scar above his left temple. He was much younger than she had anticipated—surely not above thirty-five.

'I'm Sean McGregor.' His voice was as uncompromising as his looks.

'I'm Kate Taylor,' she said evenly, refusing to be intimidated by him. 'I wrote to you.'

'So you did,' he answered in a bored voice.

'I also telephoned you,' she added frostily. 'Your . . . er . . . Maxie, the girl behind the bar, said you'd get the message.'

'I'd have thought you'd have got the message by now, Mrs Taylor,' he remarked sardonically, and turned his attention back to his game, laying a couple of crumpled banknotes on the pile in the middle of the table. 'Your twenty, and raise twenty.'

'No, that's me out,' muttered one of the other players, tossing down his cards impatiently.

'Mr McGregor,' said Kate, her rising anger adding a thread of steel to her voice, 'if your boat is fully booked, I will quite understand, although I would have appreciated it if you could have had the manners to tell me so, so that I needn't have wasted so much time. But if you're available, I would like to hire you.'

One of the other players laughed raucously. 'Hey, Sean! I bet even you don't get an offer like that every day of the week!'

The blue eyes had grown perceptibly colder. 'I'm not for hire, Mrs Taylor,' he said firmly.

'Why not?'

He dragged his attention from the card game, and let his gaze slide down over her in unhurried appraisal, lingering over every curve. A hectic flush rose to her cheeks, but her head lifted haughtily as she returned him an icy stare.

His eyes glinted with evil. 'I can think of several more interesting things to do with your body than feed it to the sharks,' he drawled in mocking insolence.

'I have no intention of allowing myself to be eaten by sharks,' she snapped. 'I'm a very experienced diver.' He lifted one quizzical eyebrow. 'As I explained in my letter, if you bothered to read it, I

worked on a number of salvage operations with my
husband, before ... before he was killed.'

'That isn't much of a recommendation,' he remarked cynically, most of his attention once again
turned to his poker hand.

'My husband was one of the foremost salvage
experts in the world,' she retorted hotly, 'and I intend
to prove it.'

'And you want me to help you do that?' he sneered.

'Yes. Though it won't be easy for me to get used to
working with second best,' she flashed, her anger
boiling over.

A shout of laughter went round the table at her
furious words, but Sean McGregor ignored it. He
calmly laid his card on the table, and drew the pile of
money towards him amid the groans of protest from
the other players.

'Well now, Mrs Taylor,' he growled, unfolding
himself lazily from his seat and stuffing his winnings
casually into the pocket of his faded denim jeans.
'You've made your pitch, and I've told you I'm not
interested. Now I suppose I'm going to have to escort
you back to your hotel.'

He took her arm in a firm grip, and she stared up at
him as he towered over her, six foot three of raw male
power. He was wearing a thick white cable-stitch
sweater that emphasised the impressive width of his
shoulders, and Kate's mouth was suddenly dry.

'That won't be necessary, Mr McGregor,' she
managed to say. 'I'm quite capable of taking care of
myself.'

He smiled down at her tauntingly, and she was
forced to concede that he was a very attractive man.
'Take a look around you, Mrs Taylor,' he remarked
drily. 'This isn't one of your pretty little English

seaside resorts, you know. If your battered body were to be found floating in the harbour in the morning, I might feel a slight twinge of conscience, since you came down here to see me.'

She was left with no alternative but to allow him to lead her back through the crowd, which gave way for him without a word on his part. 'Such chivalry,' she remarked tartly as they stepped up into the street. 'And so unexpected.'

'And so undeserved,' he returned, unruffled. 'Tell me, Mrs Taylor, are you in the habit of pursuing strange men into back-street bars?'

'Only when they're avoiding me.'

'You appear to be dangerously reckless.'

'No. Merely determined.' Her voice was as cool and distant as the night sky—a canopy of black and silver high above the Nassau rooftops.

'It seems to amount to the same thing,' he drawled lazily. 'May I ask, just as a matter of curiosity, why you're so keen on finding the *Belle Étoile* again after all these years?'

Kate stopped abruptly in the middle of the road. 'So she *is* there!' she breathed.

'Oh, she's there all right,' he confirmed grimly, drawing her out of the path of a rather irate driver who had had to slam on his brakes to avoid her. 'Did you have your doubts too, then?'

'No, of course not!' she protested quickly. 'It's just . . . Can you find her?'

He shrugged his wide shoulders in cool indifference. 'Maybe, maybe not,' he replied unhelpfully. 'She's in the middle of nowhere, and pretty heavily encrusted with coral—almost unrecognisable. And the reef will have changed a lot in the past twelve years. It won't look anything like it did then. No, I'd say the odds were against it.'

She turned her dark gaze pleadingly up to his. 'But you could try?' she implored, the words coming straight from her heart.

His eyes were as cold as flints. 'I could, but I'm not going to,' he said with an air of finality. 'Forget it, Mrs Taylor. Go back to England and play with your sea shells, or whatever it is you marine biologists do.'

'I will not!' she retorted furiously. 'If you won't help me, I shall just have to find someone else who will!'

'And how do you propose to do that?'

'I'll charter another boat, and I'll look until I find her,' she vowed with grim determination.

He swore fiercely under his breath. 'That could take months,' he argued.

'I don't care,' she asserted wildly. 'I'll stay here until all my savings are used up, and then I'll get a job, if necessary. I'll find that wreck, Mr McGregor, if it's the last thing I do!'

He glared down at her furiously. 'Damn you, Mrs Taylor,' he snapped. 'I suppose I'm going to have to help you after all. I can see you're likely to get yourself killed. At least with me you'll be comparatively safe.'

'Safe?' she echoed, sarcasm adding a cutting edge to her voice.

'Oh, yes. And I don't just mean down on the wreck.' That mocking smile had returned to curve his hard mouth. 'I do have a certain reputation to maintain,' he taunted softly. 'If my crew were to hear you screaming in the night, I'd never live it down!'

She flushed scarlet at the unmistakable implication of his words. She had barely given any consideration to the possibility of such complications arising. She would have liked to be able to tell Sean McGregor exactly where he could go, but second thoughts silenced her angry rejoinder. In spite of her reckless words, she could only afford to charter a boat for a short time, and she was due to start a teaching job in September.

Without his help, her chances of finding the *Belle Étoile* were virtually nil. However much she disliked him, she could tolerate his company for a few weeks, surely? After all, it was for Dave.

Quelling her anger with difficulty, she turned to him, her head tilted at a proud angle. 'Thank you,' she said with minimal politeness. 'When will you be ready to sail?'

'Shall we say the day after tomorrow?' he suggested. 'Ten o'clock? Since you're such an efficient little detective, I'm sure you'll be able to find my boat.'

'Fine.' They had reached the bustle of Rawson Square, and her hotel was only a few hundred yards away, on a brightly lit street. She extended her hand to him with an air of cool formality. 'I'll see you the day after tomorrow. Good night, Mr McGregor.'

'Good night, Mrs Taylor.' Long, strong fingers touched hers briefly, and he smiled that quirkily attractive smile. And then he was gone, dodging through the crowds and traffic with the lithe energy of a natural athlete.

Kate stared after him for a moment, a little bemused by the startling contrast to the image she had painted of him in her mind before she had met him. Was she taking too much of a chance, sailing alone with a man like that? There would be his crew, of course—but their loyalty would be to him.

But after all, as he had pointed out, he did have a reputation to maintain. It wouldn't do him any good if she were to complain about his behaviour to the local tourist board. No, she would be safe enough. With a careless shrug of her shoulders she turned and walked back to her hotel.

CHAPTER TWO

'GOOD morning, Mrs Taylor.'

It was ten o'clock, precise to the minute, as Kate stepped from the taxi that had brought her the short distance from her hotel. 'Good morning, Mr McGregor. We have a fine morning for sailing,' she answered, coolly ignoring the mockery in those blue eyes. She was dressed for comfort rather than sophistication, in blue jeans and a sunny yellow T-shirt, and she had made up her mind that her manner was going to be distant and formal—she was not going to let Sean McGregor goad her with his cynicism.

'We do indeed,' he agreed drily. He shouldered her heaviest bags of equipment with irritating ease, and led her along the busy quayside to the *Barracuda's* berth. Following him, her eyes widened in surprise. The *Barracuda* was not, as she had expected, a fishing-boat, but a large and luxurious motor yacht, a sleek fifty feet of gleaming white hull with a sharply raked bow that promised speed.

A young island lad, probably still in his teens, was waiting to help her aboard. 'This is Josh,' Sean told her. 'He takes care of the cooking and diving equipment, and anything else that needs doing.'

The lad beamed at her as he handed her down the short gangway. 'Welcome aboard, Miz Taylor,' he said, his accent honey soft.

'Thank you, Josh,' she smiled in reply.

'Josh's father, Joshua, looks after the boat,' Sean added. 'I suggest you stay out of his way. He's even less enthusiastic about your hare-brained scheme than I am.'

Kate was tempted to make a stinging retort, but she bit it back, swiftly recalling her good intentions. Her eyes watched him covertly from the shadow of her silky lashes, recording impressions. He was immaculately dressed this morning in white slacks and a crisp white shirt, the sleeves rolled back over strong, sunbronzed forearms. Who had washed and ironed his clothes with such loving care? she wondered tartly. The sexy blonde barmaid at the Rum Runner?

'Josh will stow your equipment,' Sean went on, putting her bags down on the aft-deck. 'I'll show you round before we cast off.'

A few steps took them down into the saloon, a comfortable, airy cabin with gleaming teak woodwork and smart coffee and cream striped upholstery. A neat corner-unit housed a televison and music centre, and there was a comprehensively stocked drinks cabinet built in under the helm seat.

'As you can see, there's plenty of room,' remarked Sean, with a sardonic inflexion in his voice. 'We won't be too close for comfort during our leisure hours.'

Kate's heart thumped unexpectedly at the thought of being too close to Sean McGregor. He was all male, and suddenly she was aware of her own femininity in a way she had never quite felt before. Fortunately he had turned away from her, and was walking forward, dipping his head automatically under the low deckhead beams. Quickly she schooled her features into a composed expression, and followed him down a couple of steps to the cabins in the bows.

'Down here we have the crew cabins and the galley,' he explained. The galley was impressive, light and well ventilated, and extremely well equipped. There was even a microwave oven. 'Guests, of course, are not expected to share the cooking. Josh does it all—you'll find him remarkably good. But any time you want coffee or a snack, just help yourself.'

Kate nodded.

'Crew cabin.' He indicated briefly towards a small cabin on the port-side, and then slid open the last door. 'My cabin.' A fleeting vision of hedonistic luxury in spice-coloured suede, and a wide oval bed, impinged startlingly on her consciousness before she turned away. Mr McGregor was no ordinary fisherman!

'Your cabin is aft,' he went on, indicating that she should lead the way back through the saloon.

The aft cabin was down another few steep steps, and the door was a little narrow, but inside it was spacious and light. There was a bunk on each side, and plenty of locker space. 'You'll be completely self-contained,' he told her, showing her a neat little bathroom with a shower cabinet. 'I'll leave you to unpack.'

She turned to face him. 'Mr McGregor,' she began determinedly, 'before we cast off, perhaps I'd better make one thing clear. I was expecting to pay only standard charter rates.'

'Of course.' His eyes glinted with cold humour. 'I wouldn't expect you to pay over the odds for what is, after all, only second best.'

So that remark had pierced his armour-plating, at least! 'I'd hardly call this boat second best,' she pointed out drily.

'Nice, isn't she?' With a taunting smile he turned away and lounged back up to the saloon, offering no explanation. Kate shrugged impatiently. If he chose to conduct his business in such an offhand manner, who was she to argue?

She glanced around the small cabin with pleasure. The headroom was a little restricted but that didn't matter. It was lit by two portholes. The colour scheme was a pale, restful grey, and the bunks were very comfortable. She chose one to sleep in, and dumped her canvas holdall on the other to unpack the few clothes she had brought.

They were mostly casual clothes—shorts and T-shirts—except for her two dresses: the pink one and one other. She didn't really know why she'd bothered to pack the second dress, but it didn't crease and it took up hardly any room. It was of a drifting, gauzy material, black with vivid splashes of fuchsia-pink in a simple, sensational style that wrapped around her waist, scooping in a deep V across the curve of her breasts and floating in soft folds to the floor.

Dave had called it her fever-dress. He had bought it for her in Nice, just a few weeks after their marriage. He had been surveying the wreck of a World War II fighter plane for a conservation society, and they had decided to snatch one precious weekend to have a honeymoon. Dave had promised her a very special weekend, and he had kept his promise. They had stayed at one of the Riviera's best hotels, with a sweeping view over the blue Mediterranean ...

Sadly she took out the little silver-framed photograph that she always kept by her bedside and set it down on the handy corner shelf above her bunk, beside her travelling-clock. She had taken that picture herself, in the grounds of the university. Dave was smiling into the camera, his red-gold hair tousled by the breeze. It seemed as though it had been only yesterday.

With a small sigh she returned to her unpacking, finishing it quickly and hurrying back up to the aft-deck as old Joshua was making ready to cast off. She offered him a friendly smile, but met only a blank look. As soon as the boat was under way he went below, stepping past her as if she wasn't there.

The narrow channel between Nassau and Paradise Island was alive with noise and colour. The local fishing-boats jostled with crowds of pleasure-craft and luxury private yachts. The *Barracuda* slipped neatly through the throng, and Kate watched as the grey stone ramparts of Fort Charlotte slid by the port rail. Beyond it the road wound and dipped under shading palms and sapodilla trees, past luxurious hotels and beaches of sun-whitened coral sand.

They were crusing at a comfortable fifteen knots, and the *Barracuda* was every bit as beautiful in action as she had looked in dock. Kate glanced up at Sean where he sat at the secondary helm-position on the flying-bridge. He was wearing a white-peaked base-ball cap, pulled low to shade his eyes, and he was steering almost lazily, one hand on the wheel, the other resting along the back of the seat in which he was lounging. And yet there was a latent power in every inch of his lean, athletic frame that suggested he was a man who was always in control.

'Coffee, Miz Taylor?' Young Josh was beaming at her from the saloon cabin.

'Oh, yes, please,' she replied, smiling back. 'And please, call me Kate.'

He nodded, delighted. 'Milk and sugar?'

'Milk, no sugar.'

'Right. I hope you like your food, Miz Kate. We're well stocked up, and I like to cook,' he told her eagerly.

She laughed. 'Good. I get very hungry when I'm diving.'

Josh looked satisfied. 'This oughtta be a real good trip,' he declared with confidence. 'The skipper, he takes care of the diving, I take care of the chow, and my pappy takes care of the boat. And you take care of yourself,' he added, suddenly grave. 'Don't you go taking no risks down on that old wreck. She's been down there a few years—she ain't going nowhere.'

'Don't worry, Josh,' Kate reassured him, smiling. 'I don't intend to take any chances.'

'I'm glad to hear it,' cut in Sean acidly as he climbed down the ladder from the flying-bridge. 'The last thing we need around a dangerous wreck like the *Belle Étoile* is an excess of amateur enthusiasm.'

'You needn't worry, Mr McGregor,' she responded coolly. 'I know what I'm doing.'

'Good. Now, what do you know about the wreck?' he enquired.

'She was two-masted brigantine, built in Tortuga,' began Kate confidently. 'Her captain was Philippe de Mercourt, one of the most notorious pirates of the Bahamas. He was sunk by the British in 1718, but it had to be hushed up, because he was related to some very important people in France, and it could have been embarrassing—there were some sort of diplomatic negotiations going on at the time. So it was put about that de Mercourt had died of the plague, and his ship burned to prevent infection,' she finished triumphantly.

'Very good,' he applauded. 'But do you know anything about the wreck itself?'

'Well, only that it's lying on the leeward side of a half-moon reef. I have the chart co-ordinates,' she told him uncertainly. 'It's about fifty feet down, and heavily encrusted with coral.'

'Right,' he agreed with a curt nod. 'And do you have any idea how many half-moon reefs there are in that area?'

'I . . . I should think there are quite a few,' replied Kate reluctantly.

'A few hundred, I shouldn't wonder,' Sean agreed. 'You'd better come and have a look at the chart.'

Kate followed him into the saloon, needled by his disparaging tone. He strolled forward, ducking smoothly under the deck-head beams, and picked up a chart from the navigator's table next to the helm position.

Old Joshua had now taken over the wheel, and Kate glanced up at him. He still seemed intent on ignoring her presence. She could almost feel his disapproval, emanating silently from every line of his back.

Sean spread the chart out on the dining table as Josh emerged from the galley with their coffee.

'There you are, Miz Kate. Is that how you like it?' asked Josh, watching as she sipped it.

'Perfect, thank you, Josh,' she told him, smiling. He nodded happily, and withdrew to his own territory for'ard.

Kate bent her head over the chart, following Sean's finger as he traced the last ill-fated voyage of the *Belle Étoile*. 'The pirate stronghold was in Nassau,' he began. 'It was just a shanty-town of driftwood and palm trees with tents made of old sails—but they had their own loose kind of organisation, for all that. In 1718 it was already breaking up—the rich pickings were elsewhere.

'When Woodes Rogers returned from England with his authority from the Crown and his offer of an amnesty, a lot of his old privateer comrades joined him, but others, led by Charles Vane and Philippe de Mercourt, fought their way out of the harbour, and got away.

'Rogers commissioned some of the reformed pirates to pursue them. They caught de Mercourt on his own, out here by Highbourne Cay, and chased him southwards over the Tongue of the Ocean. He may have been trying to make a run for it to Hispaniola. Anyway, with Hornigold's guns on his tail, he found himself facing a coral bank, here, to the south of Andros. It's riddled with channels, and he must have decided to try to outwit Hornigold's fleet by sneaking through.

'He didn't make it. The coral tore the bottom out of his boat, and she sank like a stone. De Mercourt perished; and so did most of his men. The pursuers only picked up a handful of survivors.'

Kate stared at him in amazement. 'How on earth do you know all that?' she asked.

'One of my ancestors, Robert McGregor, was commanding one of the ships in Hornigold's fleet,' he explained with little interest. 'The story's been passed down in the family for generations.'

'But . . . why haven't you ever told anyone else?'

He shrugged his wide shoulders in cool indifference. 'No one ever bothered to ask,' he said.

'But she's such a find!' she protested, aghast.

'Not really. There's nothing much to salvage—just a few rotting bits of wood, encrusted with several tons of coral.'

'Oh, come on!' Kate persisted, her dark eyes on fire. 'There's been controversy about the *Belle Étoile* ever since she sank!'

'So I believe,' he responded dispassionately. 'It really doesn't interest me. There are hundreds of wrecks around here, and every year a few more idiots get themselves killed exploring them. The *Belle Étoile* would be just another graveyard. If I had my way, she'd stay hidden for ever.'

Kate stared at him. 'Well, I suppose you have a point,' she said slowly. It was not a view that she had ever considered before. To Dave, a wreck—any wreck—was a challenge to be met and conquered, whatever the price.

Sean's blue eyes were glacial. 'Nevertheless, you're going to go ahead and look for her,' he said.

Kate sighed. 'All I know is I have to find her to prove that Dave was telling the truth,' she explained, wishing she could make him understand how important it was to her.

He leaned back in his seat, surveying her coldly. 'Very well,' he rapped. 'Let's get a few ground rules established then, shall we? We don't dive if I say we don't, and we surface when I say so. No arguments. Is that clear?'

Kate glanced at him questioningly. 'You're diving with me?'

'You don't expect me to let you dive alone, do you?'

'Well, I suppose . . .'

'It's inclusive in the charter rates,' he assured her cynically. 'It's very bad for business to lose a customer.'

'I see,' she responded tautly. 'Well, in that case, thank you, Mr McGregor. You certainly offer a comprehensive service.'

'We aim to please.' His eyes were coolly mocking. 'One more thing,' he added in a sardonic tone that robbed his words of any warmth. 'You and I are going to be diving together in some quite dangerous waters. Do you think we could try to put our relationship on a slightly more friendly footing? A little mutual trust would go a long way towards helping us both survive this crazy trip.'

'By all means, Mr McGregor,' Kate responded with dignity. 'I admit that I was annoyed by your bad manners in not returning my calls, but I'm perfectly prepared to put that behind us.'

He seemed mildly amused by her reluctant concession. 'Good,' he said. 'Shall we begin by dropping the formality? My name's Sean.'

He was smiling that oddly attractive smile again, and Kate found herself suddenly unable to reply. She transferred her attention quickly to the chart spread in front of her. 'How long will it take us to get there . . . er . . . Sean?' she managed to say in a voice that wavered oddly.

'We'll be there by late afternoon,' he told her. 'We'll anchor here, close to the main island, and tomorrow we can go out and have a look at the coral bank.'

'You don't know exactly where the wreck is lying, then?' she asked.

'Within a few hundred yards,' he responded with infuriating insouciance. 'But among the coral reefs that might as well be fifty miles. She isn't going to be easy to find.'

'I'm quite aware of the difficulties,' she told him, her voice now as cool as his. 'I've worked on several salvage operations.'

He was sipping his coffee, and watching her thoughtfully. 'How long have you been diving?' he asked.

'Since I was a child.'

His eyebrows lifted fractionally. 'Oh? Dave didn't teach you, then?'

Again Kate detected that hint of antipathy in his

tone, and glanced up at him questioningly. 'No, he didn't,' she answered. Her eyes searched his, but that cool façade gave nothing away. 'He ... never mentioned you to me, you know,' she remarked cautiously. 'Did you know him well?'

'Not particularly.' He began folding the chart. 'How are you going to go about salvaging this wreck—if we find it?'

'Oh, I know I won't be able to undertake a big operation,' she said, 'I'm just hoping I'll be able to take some photographs and measurements, and maybe bring up a couple of things if I'm lucky.'

His expression was again cynical. 'Do you really think it's worth it? Risking your life to find some ancient wreck that's only of interest to maybe a dozen people?'

'Of course it's worth it,' she insisted without hesitation. 'Finding the *Belle Étoile* was Dave's proudest achievement. I'm not going to let anyone take that away from him!'

He laughed scornfully. 'Oh, I get it,' he sneered. 'You're fighting some sort of duel for the honour of the late great Dave Taylor.'

The sarcasm in his voice lashed her anger to white heat. 'He doesn't need me to fight for his honour!' she snapped. 'His reputation was above reproach.'

'You really believe that, don't you?' he mused. 'He could do no wrong in your eyes.'

'That's right!' she flashed furiously. 'He was brilliant.'

Their eyes clashed, hers blazing, his ice-cool. After a moment he shrugged and stood up, picking up her coffee-cup. 'You might as well take it easy while you can. You'll be out of the way up on the flying-bridge.'

She wasn't ready to finish the argument so abruptly,

but he had already gone down the steps that led to the galley. She got up impatiently and walked out on to the aft-deck, and stood watching the silver wake unfurl behind the yacht. It was rather odd, she reflected, that Dave had never spoken of Sean McGregor—she would have thought he would make a powerful impression, even on a brief aquaintance.

With a wry smile she acknowledged the answer to her own question. Dave would have regarded the finding of the *Belle Étoile* as *his* triumph—which indeed it was. Sean had plainly never known the importance of the *Belle Étoile* until Dave had told him. Part of the skill of a salvage expert was in using local knowledge to pinpoint the position of a wreck, and in finding a man who was descended from one of the original seamen in that long-ago fleet, Dave had accomplished a feat no less impressive than that of locating the sunken ship itself.

It was understandable, perhaps, that Sean wouldn't see it that way. Probably the two men had quar-relled—she could well imagine that there would have been an undercurrent of rivalry between them. And what of Sean himself? How did he come to own such a superb boat as the *Barracuda*? There must be a good deal of money in the charter business in Nassau! Maybe he had even won her in a game of cards?

With a dismissive shrug she set the thought aside, and climbed the ladder to the flying-bridge, where she could strip down to her bikini and sunbathe in comparative privacy. Her mind drifted to thoughts of the task that lay ahead. The *Belle Étoile* had lain on the sea floor for more than two hundred and fifty years. She would be very hard to find. Dave's log-book described how she lay deeply embedded in the reef—and Kate knew well the frustration of searching for a wreck in such conditions. Every stand of coral seemed to hide a cannon or an anchor.

At least in the crystal clear waters of the Bahamas, visibility was excellent, but at a depth of fifty feet they would only be able to stay on the bottom for forty-five minutes—or a little longer if they dived twice a day. Then there were the dangers: from the coral itself, which could inflict a nasty graze on an incautious diver, from jellyfish and sea-urchins; and that nerve-snapping danger always present in warm seas—sharks.

It was reassuring to know that Sean would be diving with her. Much as she disliked him on a personal level, she felt instinctively that he would be a competent diving buddy. When there was so much that could go wrong, that mutual trust he had spoken of was essential. Even the most straightforward dive could end in disaster if there should be any carelessness.

Long ago, years before she had met him, Dave had almost been killed in a diving accident that had claimed the lives of two of his friends. He had managed to save a third, sharing the last of his own precious air to bring him to the surface. And all because the air-tanks had not been properly filled. The other three had been inexperienced divers, and had panicked when their air had run out—and panic was diver's worst enemy.

The afternoon was becoming a little tedious. The enforced inactivity after all the excitement of preparing for the trip was making her restless. When she heard Josh setting out lunch on the aft-deck, she pulled her clothes on over her bikini and went down to join them.

To starboard lay a low island, thickly tangled with mangrove jungle, slashed by deep, mysterious creeks.

Along its coast a ribbon of dancing green water betrayed the presence of a coral reef. The sea was a deep, majestic royal blue, and the surging power of the water under the hull suggested that there were many fathoms beneath them. 'Where are we, Josh?' she asked.

'We're running down the Tongue of the Ocean,' Josh told her. 'It's real deep—over two miles in places.'

'That's deep!' Kate agreed, her eyes widening. 'Is that Andros Island, then?'

'Yes, Miz Kate. But you don't want to go there,' he added, lowering his voice theatrically. 'It's an evil place.'

Kate gazed out over the water towards the island. It had a strange haunting beauty that made it difficult to dismiss Josh's superstitious warning entirely.

'Oh, Josh, don't be silly,' she protested, her voice shaking a little. 'How can it be evil?'

'Chickcharnies,' he uttered in an awed whisper.

'Chickcharnies? What are they?'

'They have three toes, and red eyes, and they hang by their tails in cottonwood trees,' Josh intoned darkly. Kate burst out laughing. 'You mustn't laugh, Miz Kate,' Josh protested with solemn gravity. 'You laugh at a chickcharnie he twist your head right around backwards on your shoulders.'

Kate looked at him curiously. 'Do you believe in them?' she asked, a little afraid that she might be offending him by not taking him seriously.

'Of course.' He crept towards her with clawed fingers outstretched, his eyes full of youthful mischief. 'My mammy used to tell me about them when I was little.'

Kate dodged away from him, laughing—and

gasped in shock as she collided with a hard body. She glanced up to find herself looking into a pair of cool blue eyes.

'You shouldn't fool around like that on a boat, you know,' he reminded her, an ironic inflection in his voice. 'You might fall overboard.'

'I ... I'm sorry,' she stammered. 'Josh was just telling me about the chickcharnies.' Her heart was pounding with shock from the unexpected contact, but if Sean noticed he chose to ignore it.

'You're more likely to encounter a Russian submarine,' he told her drily. 'There's an American weapons-testing station up the coast.'

Kate shuddered. 'Heavens! I think I'd prefer the chickcharnies!'

'Oh, I don't think we'll have much trouble from either,' he drawled indifferently, and settled himself opposite her at the small table. Josh had cooked up a delicious risotto of red snapper with peas and rice, seasoned with peppers, and for a sweet produced ice cream covered with grated fresh coconut.

'Mmmm. That was superb!' sighed Kate, leaning back against the rail and closing her eyes. 'When I arranged to hire your boat, you didn't tell me that the food was going to be such a bonus.'

'You seem to have left a great deal to chance when you were planning this expedition,' Sean remarked.

She opened her eyes and glared at him in indignation. 'I didn't have much choice,' she told him, her voice sharp. 'I couldn't afford a lot of elaborate organisation.'

'Don't you have a father or a brother or something, to stop you taking such foolish risks?'

'It isn't a foolish risk,' she retorted, pride lifting her head. 'I know what I'm doing. And my father never interferes. I'm a grown woman.'

His eyes took a lazy survey of her slender body, and her cheeks flushed a heated red. 'I can see you are,' he drawled insolently. 'All the more reason why you should be more careful.'

She tucked her feet up on the seat, hugging her knees in defence. 'Mr McGregor,' she protested, her voice shaking, 'Please remember that ours is purely a business relationship.'

He smiled that taunting smile. 'Of course,' he conceded mockingly. 'What else?' He eased himself lazily to his feet. 'Now if you'll excuse me,' he added, 'I think I'll do a little sunbathing myself. If anyone wants me, I'll be up front.'

As he made his way along the narrow side-deck towards the bows he unfastened his shirt and pulled it off. His back rippled with smooth muscles beneath skin that glowed bronze and healthy. Kate blinked, suddenly realising that she was staring at him. She pulled herself together sharply, and hurried down to her cabin to fetch a book, and then climbed up to the flying-bridge to settle down on the cushions she had left in the floor-well to continue her sunbathing.

She spent the rest of the afternoon in the sunshine, trying to read, but distracted by the ospreys and pelicans squabbling over the fish brought to the surface in the *Barracuda's* churning wake. As the sun began to sink lower in the flawless blue sky, they rounded the southernmost tip of Andros, and began to sail towards a cluster of small cays offshore.

Sean steered the yacht skilfully through the narrow channels between the reefs that fringed the low, green islands, and they dropped anchor in a peaceful lagoon. As the steady throb of the engines died, a noisy silence of shrill bird calls drifted out from the thickets of coco-

plums and sea-grapes that grew right down to the long,
glistening white beaches.

The water was an incredibly clear, opaline blue, and
looked so shallow that Kate felt as though she would
be able to wade on the sandy bottom—but she knew
that the impression was deceptive, and that the lagoon
was probably several metres deep.

'Dinner'll be ready in half an hour, Miz Kate,'
announced Josh.

'Fine, Josh. It looks as though we're going to have a
peaceful night.' There was hardly a breath of wind,
and not a cloud marred the flawless perfection of the
sky.

'Sure thing,' agreed Josh. 'Looks like we could get
the green flash tonight.'

'The green flash? What is that?' asked Kate
curiously.

'It's an unusual refraction of the light, as the sun
sets,' Sean told her as he sauntered out on to the deck.
'It only happens when it's very clear, like tonight.'

'It's very lucky,' Josh added eagerly. 'Especially for
lovers.'

Kate turned to gaze out at the finely drawn line
where the sea met the sky. There was a strange
stillness in the air, as if the whole world had paused to
watch breathlessly. The sun sank slowly down the sky,
turning the sea to a crucible of liquid gold. And then in
the last split second before it slid majestically below
the horizon, there was a dazzling flash of purest
emerald light, there and gone faster than a wink.

Kate let go her breath in a soundless sigh. She was
aware of Sean standing behind her—quite close,
maybe eighteen inches away—and an odd shimmer of
heat ran through her, though he had not touched her.
'I ... I think I'll go and change for dinner,' she

mumbled, and hurried quickly down to her cabin.

She couldn't understand why she should react like that to him. But he made her nervous, with his cool self-assurance and mocking façade. Was there a real man in there somewhere, capable of human warmth? She shivered. Perhaps it would be better if she didn't find out!

CHAPTER THREE

THE *Barracuda* was moving forward very slowly, her powerful twin diesel engines edging her through the reef at a speed that only just overcame the drag of the treacherous currents through the maze of channels. Old Joshua was stationed in the bows, Josh was on the port-quarter, and Kate had the starboard.

The sky was a flawless blue, wisped with just a few stray clouds in the distance. The sea was as smooth as silk, an incredibly clear crystal green, and the sandy bottom swathed in acres of sea-grass, was visible fifty feet below the hull.

All around, the sharp coral, so beautiful and yet so dangerous, waited for the slightest error to throw the yacht on to its merciless teeth. But there were no errors. Up on the flying-bridge Sean steered with faultless precision through the narrow channel, one hand on the wheel, the other holding the headset of the echo-sounder to his ear.

Kate could only admire his skill. The coral bank, some five miles south of Andros, was several square miles in area. In places the coral broke the surface, glistening gold and white in the sun, but most of it lay just below the dancing green water.

When the mid-morning sun was shining down on a tranquil sea, as today, it was possible to pick out the sandy passages through the reefs. But in poor light or rougher weather it would be a death trap. Kate shuddered, thinking of those desperate men who had braved this path rather than surrender, in a craft not

41

much bigger than the *Barracuda*, but lacking the hair-trigger manoeuvrability of the modern boat.

At last Sean yelled, 'Okay,' and cut the engines. Josh raced back to drop the stern-anchor as his father dropped the other from the bows. Kate straightened her back with a sign of relief, and looked around. The sea was a tapestry of blues and greens, laced with tiny white wavelets where the water broke over the reefs.

'We'll dive in half an hour,' said Sean, climbing down the ladder to the aft-deck. 'The sun will still be high enough to give us a good chance of seeing anything there is to see.'

'You're sure this is the right reef?' she enquired, torn between hope of finding the wreck, and a desire to see Sean's cool self-assurance shaken. But his response frustrated both objects.

'No,' he said indifferently. 'We'll spend a week here, and if we find nothing we'll move on. I warned you, we might never find it.' He strolled into the saloon, quite unperturbed by the possibility of failure.

Kate went down to her cabin, and spent a while carefully re-reading Dave's log-book, memorising his descriptions of the first appearance of the wreck. When she climbed back up on deck sometime later, she found that Sean had assembled a collapsible shark-cage and slung it over the stern on heavy-gauge nylon ropes. He had rigged a pulley-system over the transom, and wound the ropes on a small winch.

'Very good,' she applauded, glancing over the rail at the cage resting on the sandy bottom of the lagoon.

Sean glanced at her, his blue eyes humourless. 'At the first sign of trouble, we retreat to the cage,' he told her in a voice that was accustomed to being obeyed without question.

'Yes, sir,' she responded demurely.

He slanted her a warning glance. 'You're taking no stupid risks off my boat. I intend to see that you get back to Nassau in one piece.'

'I assure you that if I wind up as a shark's dinner I won't hold you responsible,' she vowed solemnly, hand on heart.

'That isn't very funny.'

'All right!' she snapped, needled by his infuriating manner. 'I'm quite well aware of the dangers. But I'm responsible for my own actions. I don't see why anyone should blame you if things go wrong.'

'Don't you?'

'Oh, I forgot,' she sneered, beginning to lose her temper. 'It would be bad for business, wouldn't it? Heaven forbid that anything should tarnish the shining reputation of the great Sean McGregor!'

He rounded on her, as angry and dangerous as a storm at sea. She stepped back in shock. 'I ... I'm sorry,' she gasped, 'I didn't mean that. Of course I'll be careful.'

He glared at her, his anger ebbing away slowly. 'Go and get ready,' he ordered brusquely. 'You'd better put your full wet-suit on—it'll be cold at fifty feet, and the coral's pretty sharp.'

Kate accepted his instructions meekly. She had been wrong to laugh about the shark-cage—it was an essential precaution. The greatest risk to a diver when there were sharks around was, she knew, the moment of climbing out of the water. She could not deny Sean's competence, whatever other flaws there were in his character.

She hurried down to her cabin, and changed into the sleek-fitting swimsuit she always wore beneath her neoprene wet-suit. When she got back on deck, Sean was already suited-up. She rolled on her leggings and

zipped herself into her jacket, and carefully tested her
air-tanks before letting Josh lift them on to her back.

She fastened the harness comfortably over her
buoyancy jacket, and then as Josh handed her the rest
of her equipment she checked each piece before
putting it on, as her grandfather had trained her—
weight-belt, diving knife, depth-guage. Out of the
corner of her eye she noted with satisfaction that Sean
was following the same disciplined practice.

When she was ready, she turned to Sean with a
bright smile. 'Good luck,' she said cheerfully.

'Luck doesn't enter into it,' he responded coldly. 'I
prefer to trust my eyes, and this.' He was holding a
cartridge-loaded shark stick, and for an angry
moment Kate glared at him, resenting his chilly
efficiency. No one would be less like Dave. But she
had to acknowledge that if anything went wrong her
life could depend on that efficiency. So without
another word she climbed over the transom and down
the ladder to the swim platform.

She leaned into the water to rinse her face-mask and
flippers before putting them on, and then glanced
across at Sean, who was now beside her. 'Ready?' she
asked.

'Ready,' he concurred.

She fitted her snorkel into her mouth, and rolled
neatly backwards into the water, somersaulting away
from the boat. She was tumbling in a confusing world
of luminous green and shining bubbles, with a
cacophony of roarings and metalic clankings in her
ears. She uncurled herself slowly, wanting to laugh at
the wobbling, saucer-shaped bubbles in front of her
eyes. She let herself drift to the surface, popping the
bubbles with her finger as she went and watching as

each one shattered into a dozen smaller replicas of itself.

She broke the surface, tossing back her hair, and cleared the water from her face mask and snorkel-tube. Josh was waving to her from the deck, and she gave him the okay sign, and turned to Sean as he came up beside her.

'Okay?' he asked. She nodded. 'We'll snorkel over to the reef and mark our starting point,' he said. 'You lead.'

She rolled over and began to fin slowly towards the reef. As they reached it, Sean dropped the first of the red marker-buoys. 'Okay,' he said. 'Be careful of the fire-coral, there's a lot of it about.'

'I will,' she promised. 'I make it twelve twenty-seven,' she added, glancing at her diving watch.

'Right,' agreed Sean, checking his watch against hers. 'We come up at twelve minutes past one.'

Kate set her marker, and then fitted her air-valve into her mouth and turned on the supply. They exchanged okay signs, and then she dipped smoothly under the water and began to fin slowly down to where the buoy had dropped next to the reef.

The coral was like an incredible garden, elegant clusters of stag- or elk-horn, intricate twists of brain-coral, leaflike plates of agaricia. It was a far more interesting world than the one she had known back at her grandfather's villa on the Mediterranean. There seemed to be every type of coral she had ever heard of, as well as sponges, prickly sea-urchins, frilly sea-slugs, and mollusc shells glowing iridescent in the filtering sunlight.

The reef was alive with the waving fronds of sea anemones, and the feathery pastel-coloured rosettes of gill-worms. Schools of jewel-bright damsel-fish and wrasses flashed by, disturbed occasionally by the long, lethal shape of a hunting barracuda, spreading alarm. Suddenly a piece of sponge moved, and Kate wanted to laugh again, realising that it was not sponge at all, but a bat-fish, spectacularly ugly in its disguise.

It would be easy to drift around all day, there was so much to see. But she had a job to do, and resolutely she turned her attention to a detailed inspection of the coral formations along the base of the reef. Here on the leeward side, little of the coral was still actively growing—the still water close to the sandy bottom did not carry enough of the essential oxygen. But the nooks and corners of a sunken ship could be an oasis, allowing the coral to proliferate—so that was one of the clues they were looking for, an unusually rich growth of live coral among the debris.

Kate searched meticulously, tapping with her diving-knife to break open any likely-looking clumps. She noticed that while Sean was also searching, he was constantly alert to everything in the waters around them, leaving her free to concentrate on her work. But she found nothing, and as they came to the end of their allotted time, Sean touched her arm, and pointed upwards.

She nodded, and, checking the position of the dark shadow of the boat's hull against the sapphire glow of the surface, began to fin slowly upwards, allowing herself to drift at the same rate as the silver bubbles of air she was breathing out.

Sean surfaced close beside her. 'Okay?' he asked.

'Okay.' She had to set aside her disappointment at their lack of success. After all, that was only their first dive—she couldn't expect too much luck.

'Hungry?' asked Sean.

'Starving!'

'Josh will have lunch ready as soon as you've showered,' he promised.

She glanced round for the *Barracuda*, a gleaming white cliff fifty yards away, the blue and white diving pennant fluttering cheerfully from the flagpole on the flying-bridge. 'Right. See you on board,' she said, and began to fin lazily back towards the swim platform.

Josh leaned over the transom to help her as she hoisted herself up the ladder, and handed her a welcome cup of hot chocolate before turning his attention to helping her out of her diving gear. 'I'll rinse everything for you,' he offered.

'Thanks, Josh.' She wriggled out of her wetsuit and wrapped herself up in a big, fluffy towel as Sean joined her on the deck. Lounging back on one of the cushioned seats that ran along the side-rails, she sipped her chocolate with a contented sigh.

'Tired?' asked Sean with a rare smile.

She glanced up at him. 'A little,' she admitted. 'I haven't dived much since . . . since last year.' Without warning a tear welled into the corner of her eye, and she brushed it away quickly.

'You haven't really got over it, have you?' His voice was surprisingly gentle.

She shook her head. 'I don't suppose I ever will,' she whispered thickly.

'What will you do when this is all over?'

'What do you mean?' she asked blankly.

'Don't you have any future beyond this crusade of yours? Some fulfilling career mapped out? A new romance on the horizon?'

'No . . . I mean . . . I hadn't really given it much thought,' she admitted, avoiding his eyes. 'I've got a job teaching in a big comprehensive school, but I can't say I'm looking forward to it very much.'

'You don't enjoy teaching?'

'Well, I think I would,' she mused, 'if only the children were interested in what I was teaching them. But I went to see the place just before the end of last term, and it was horrific. There are nearly fifteen hundred kids in the school, all rampaging around this huge concrete bunker of a place—the building's so badly designed, it's no wonder the kids hate it. The architect ought to go to prison for building a school like that!'

He laughed. 'What would you rather be doing?'

She leaned back against the rail and closed her eyes, enjoying the moment of blissful dreams. 'Sitting on a boat in the sunshine, and diving among the most beautiful coral reefs in the world,' she said with a wistful sigh.

'Well, schoolteachers have long holidays,' he pointed out by way of compensation.

'Yes—but I'm never going to be able to afford a trip like this again. It's only the advance from the magazine that's made it possible.'

'Maybe you'll find a millionaire to marry.'

Kate slanted him a glance of wry humour. 'In Peckham? And anyway, I don't want to get married again.'

'Not even to a millionaire?'

'Especially to a millionaire!' she laughed. 'I think I'll go and have my shower now. See you later.'

Kate spent another lazy afternoon sunbathing on the flying-bridge, and then joined Sean on the aft-deck for dinner. They dined, alone as usual, and she found herself wishing that Josh and his father would join them—it was nerve-racking to have to spend so much time with Sean, struggling to maintain a flow of casual small talk.

It was a beautiful evening, the moon reflected like liquid silver in the dark, tranquil water. 'Peaceful, isn't it?' remarked Sean, stretching lazily.

'Oh ... yes,' she agreed, aware of a strange tension inside her. She stood up, and moved over to the rail. 'Can you navigate by the stars?' she asked him.

'Not in these waters—they're far too dangerous,' he answered easily. 'In open waters—yes, I could. But I prefer to rely on satellite navigation.'

She laughed. 'How prosaic!'

'But much safer.'

Yes, much safer, she thought wildly as he moved to the rail beside her. Stardust could have a very odd effect on the heartbeat! But she stood her ground resolutely. After all, so what if the night was ... undeniably romantic? She was immune—especially in present company.

Even so, her voice didn't sound quite natural to her own ears as she asked, 'Which is the Pole Star? Do you find it the same way you do in England?'

'Yes. Find the Great Bear first,' he told her.

She scanned the heavens, looking for patterns. 'I've got it,' she announced triumphantly. 'There it is. Which is Cassiopeia?'

Sean touched her shoulders lightly, moving her to face exactly the right way, and pointed over her shoulder so that she could look along his arm to find the constellation. She could feel herself trembling at his closeness, and tried to move away, but his fingers still gripped her shoulders and held her still.

'Look there,' he said, pointing to three stars lower in the sky. 'That's Orion. And there, see—just above them—that one's called Betelgeuse.'

'Beetle juice?' she repeated incredulously. 'No, I don't believe you. It couldn't be!'

'Oh, I assure you, it's quite true.' He spelled the name for her. She glanced up at him, laughing—and her heart thudded a warning as their eyes met. She stepped away from him quickly, her arms wrapped protectively around her body. 'What's wrong?' he asked, his voice softly taunting.

'Nothing,' she answered, a little too quickly. 'It's just . . . just that it's getting a little chilly now.'

'Oh. I thought perhaps you were worrying about what we might come up against down on the reef.'

'Of course not,' she countered, pride lifting her head. 'I'm not afraid.'

'Well, you damned well should be. This is going to be no picnic, you know.'

She met his eyes defiantly. 'Of course, if you think you can't manage it, we can always go back to Nassau, and I can hire another boat,' she reminded him in a mocking tone.

'Oh, I can manage it,' he returned, his voice soft with anger. 'But can you?' Without waiting for an answer, he turned and went back into the saloon.

They worked their way out along both arms of the reef, searching carefully, but they found nothing. On the sixth day, Sean went out in the inflatable tender and returned to report that there was another reef a little to the south-west that had possibilities, and that the channel to it was clear.

The following day they took a rest from diving, relocating the *Barracuda* close to the second reef while the sun was at its highest. They had been diving twice a day to maximise bottom-time, and Kate found it exhausting—not that she would have let Sean guess that.

After the sparks that had flown on the first couple of days, things had settled down a little. Sean was beginning to thaw—once or twice he had even made her laugh with his dry sense of humour—but Kate was still rather wary of him. And yet when they were diving together they seemed to share an uncanny communication that was almost telepathic.

Sean had certainly proved his worth as a diving buddy. She felt utterly safe with him, knowing that he was aware of everything around them, confident that whatever arose, he could deal with it. It was nice to be able to relax and trust a diving companion. Her grandfather had been like that, with a healthy respect for the potential dangers even in such clear, shallow water.

Dave had often had his mind too fully occupied with whatever he was studying to take note of such vital matters as depth or drift, and it had often been up to Kate to remind him of the passage of time. And he had taken risks, too—risks that had sometimes frightened Kate. But that was what had made him the best in his field.

It was a long, lazy afternoon, with nothing to do but lie in the sun. But Kate couldn't relax. She was all too conscious that Sean was lying just a few feet away from her, down on the striped air cushion that fitted over the coach roof of the forward cabins.

She couldn't help wondering about him, about the way he lived. He was a seaman to his fingertips, completely at home out here on the water, at the helm of his boat. And what of the other part of his life, when he was not at sea? She shuddered at the memory of that dim, smoky bar. Why would a man who could afford to run a yacht as beautiful as the *Barracuda* choose to rent rooms in such a disreputable place?

And did he live there alone? she wondered. Her mouth curved into a cynical smile as she remembered the stunning Maxie. No, she couldn't imagine that Sean McGregor would stint himself of female companionship. He was the type of man who made women weak, with his level blue eyes and hard-muscled body.

A strange compulsion made her sit up, and creep silently forward to peer down from the flying-bridge. Sean was stretched out on his back, his head resting on his folded hands, his white-peaked baseball-cap tipped down over his eyes. He was wearing only a pair of faded denim shorts that looked as though he'd been born in them, and the muscular length of his body was lightly scattered with rough hair, bleached almost white by the sun.

Kate watched as his powerful chest rose and fell with the deep steady rhythm of his breathing. She scarcely dared breathe herself in case he should hear her and look up. There was a latent strength in that hard, masculine body, even in total relaxation, and it fascinated her. She wondered what it would be like to touch those smooth muscles, to trail her fingers through that smattering of rough curls at the base of his throat . . .

She turned away abruptly, her heart racing. What was she doing, thinking like that about a man who was almost a stranger? Quickly she pulled on her T-shirt, and hurried down to her cabin. A warm shower eased the tensions out of her body. She felt as if the ashes of a dozen emotions were washing down the drain with the water. She had felt more since her arrival in the Bahamas than she had for months—anger, exhilaration, sadness, guilt . . .

Her reaction to Sean's forceful male presence almost shocked her. She could no longer ignore the tentative stirring of desire inside her. She was going to have to get a firm grip on herself, or he was going to start picking up signals she didn't want to transmit.

She had little doubt that he would coolly take every advantage of her, if she let him. And it took little imagination to guess that the sort of man who frequented sleazy waterfront bars like the Rum Runner would *not* be the sort to treat a relationship with a woman very seriously.

She stepped from the shower, and vigorously rubbed herself dry. The big, rough towel made her skin tingle and glow, and as she opened the clothes-locker she caught her breath—there was a full-length mirror inside the door, and she had a sudden, startling view of herself, naked. She stared at the reflection, at the soft, slender curves of her body, and a hollow little ache began inside her.

An image drifted into her mind of a long, lithe, sun-bronzed body, and she quivered in shock. What was happening to her? She had dreamed such dreams before, but it had always been Dave who had moved through them—ever since she had first met him. Sean had no right to trespass on such private territory.

She shook her head impatiently. It was only because they were confined so closely on the boat that he could unsettle her so. But he could only temporarily disturb her peace of mind. In a few weeks the trip would be over, and she could go back to England, and forget that Sean McGregor had ever existed. And thank goodness for that!

She turned away from the mirror, and reached into the locker. Her hand hesitated, momentarily, over the black dress, but then she pulled out a pair of white slacks and a soft pink sweater, and closed the door firmly. Maybe it was only natural, after all, that she should feel the occasional tug of physical need—she was young, and her husband had been snatched away from her when she had barely begun to learn the pleasures of love.

But there was no need for her to indulge such thoughts, she scolded herself briskly. It would be as though she were being unfaithful to Dave. She had a job to do, and she was going to see it through. She could cope with Sean McGregor. After all, it was only for a few short weeks.

They dined, as usual, on the aft-deck, alone. In spite of her good intentions, Kate felt herself all too aware of a tension between them, a tension that had its roots in the primeval forces that could flow between a man and a woman.

But Sean seemed indifferent to it, if he sensed it at all, as he lounged back, totally at ease, on one of the bench-seats. He was wearing a faded shirt of pale blue cotton, with the sleeves torn out, and the muscles of his arms were smooth and powerful beneath his gleaming bronzed skin. He was describing to Kate how he hunted and caught the shark that infested the warm, tranquil waters of the Bahamas, his voice coolly matter-of-fact as he spoke of things she knew must be very dangerous.

'Aren't you ever afraid?' she asked, grudging the respect he commanded.

'Of course,' he said readily. 'The man who's never afraid is a fool. That's where the excitement comes from—pitting your skill against the forces of nature.' A faintly sardonic gleam lit his blue eyes. 'But I always weigh up the odds,' he added deliberately. 'I've no interest in being a dead hero.'

Kate bridled at once. 'What do you mean by that?' she demanded angrily. He shrugged, his smile mocking her. 'Are you talking about Dave?'

'I never said so,' he pointed out. 'You thought of it.'

'Dave *was* a hero,' she threw at him. 'He was the bravest man I ever met!'

'And you were crazy about him?'

'Yes.'

He gave a hollow laugh. 'Yeah. Crazy. And you're still crazy. Like an adolescent with a crush.'

'I wouldn't expect you to understand,' she threw at him. 'What on earth would you know about love?'

'I certainly don't recognise the emotion you're suffering from,' he returned.

'Of course not. I dare say your experience of love consists of a dizzying roundabout of one-night stands.'

His eyes glinted coldly angry, and she felt his gaze linger in insolent appraisal over the soft, feminine contours of her body.

'Why should I stick around any longer when I can get all I want in one night?' he drawled with chilling cynicism.

Kate felt her heart thudding painfully. 'You're . . . you're despicable,' she retaliated hotly.

He lifted one eyebrow in mocking enquiry. 'I thought our relationship was strictly business,' he drawled with a taunting smile. 'Why should you be concerned with my morals—or lack of them?'

She leapt to her feet, her self-control snapping. 'I assure you I really couldn't care less how you choose to live,' she spat at him. 'You stick to women like that . . . that Maxie of yours. Personally, I wouldn't touch you with a barge-pole.'

She turned him an aloof shoulder, and stalked back into the saloon, his mocking laughter echoing in her ears. She stormed down to her cabin and slammed the door fiercely, and threw herself on to the bunk.

She hated him! How dare he look at her like that, as if he were judging what she looked like without her clothes on? Maybe the sort of women he was used to were quite willing to settle for a one-night stand. Well, she certainly wasn't like that—and if Sean McGregor thought he could enliven the trip with a little idle dalliance, he was in for a surprise!

Her glance fell upon the photograph of Dave, and she picked it up. A small tear trickled from the corner of her eye. 'Oh, I wish you were here,' she whispered. 'You'd teach him a few manners.'

CHAPTER FOUR

THEY reconnoitred the whole length of the reef on the following day, and then went back to study more closely anything that had attracted their attention. But in five days of diving they found nothing, and Kate had to struggle to keep herself from becoming despondent as day after day passed without success.

With nothing to do but lie around in the sun when she wasn't diving, she was finding it difficult to channel her thoughts, and more and more she found them turning to Sean. But set against her growing attraction towards him was a nagging curiosity about his evident dislike of Dave.

She couldn't really make sense of it. He had accused her of believing Dave could do no wrong, but that wasn't strictly true. She had known that Dave could sometimes be a little wild, a little impulsive. But if he was quick to quarrel, he was even quicker to make up, apologising so generously that there was never any rancour borne. Everyone had liked him—except Sean McGregor. Why?

She would have liked to ask him, but somehow she didn't know how to broach the subject. Maybe Joshua could have shed some light, but he continued to ignore her. So she tried to probe young Josh. 'I expect you were too young to have been with Sean and my husband the first time they found this wreck we're looking for?' she suggested as a beginning.

But before Josh could answer, Sean intervened as if on cue. 'Josh, come and give me a hand with this distribution panel, would you?' he called from the saloon.

'Sure, skipper, coming right along,' Josh called back cheerfully. "Scuse me, Miz Kate,' he added with an apologetic smile.

Kate pulled a wry face as he went off to obey Sean's summons, then with a careless shrug of her shoulders she climbed the ladder to the flying-bridge. She'd find out sooner or later. For now, she was going to settle down on the cushions in the floor-well for a few hours' relaxation in the afternoon sunshine.

She felt so comfortable in her privacy there now that she had taken to discarding her bikini top to avoid getting pale marks on her tan. She scrunched her sun-hat well down on her head to protect the nape of her neck, and laying her forehead on her arms let herself drift on the fringes of sleep.

Below her on the aft-deck she could hear Sean talking quietly to Josh. Without troubling to catch the words, she let herself listen to the sound of his voice. It was a strangely attractive voice, deep and slightly roughened, as if years of sea air and smoky bar rooms had sandpapered his vocal cords.

The sun was hot on her back, warming her body right through to her bones. The voices ceased, and she heard the men's footsteps moving back through the saloon cabin. Restlessly she turned on to her back. Deep inside her that uncomfortable ache of emptiness had started again, in spite of all her efforts to ignore it.

As the sun caressed her skin she began to slide into a world of half-dreams, where her rational mind loosed its hold on her fantasies. She saw a lithe, muscular body—blue eyes that taunted her—a hard mouth that could curve into a fascinating smile ... A soft, languorous sigh escaped her lips, and she smiled secretly at the vivid images that were swirling in her brain.

A sound close beside her startled her, and she opened eyes still lustrous from her dreams to find Sean climbing the ladder from the aft-deck, not troubling to disguise his appreciative survey of every slender curve of her body.

'Excuse me,' he drawled lazily, 'I just came up to check the radar-scanner.'

'Go away!' Kate sat up quickly, her face scarlet as she hugged her arms protectively over her naked breasts.

'I won't be a minute,' he answered, stepping on to the flying-bridge. She stared up at him, struggling to clarify in her mind where dreams had ended and reality began. His blue eyes flickered over her in mocking amusement. 'What's the matter?' he asked teasingly.

She lifted her head, returning his gaze with as much dignity as she could muster. 'I suppose it didn't occur to you to call out or something?' she managed to say. 'Josh always does.'

'I'm sorry,' he responded in the most unapologetic voice she had ever heard. 'I didn't realise you'd be embarrassed. Most girls sunbathe topless these days.'

'Yes, well—maybe on a public beach,' she protested. 'But that's different.'

One eyebrow lifted fractionally. 'Is it? Why?'

'You know why!' she cried, her eyes flickering with angry lights. 'There are more people around.'

'Instead of just me,' he finished, the intimate tone of his voice confirming that he knew exactly what the difference was.

'Mr McGregor, you promised me when I hired this

boat that I would be safe,' she reminded him, her voice quavering.

His mouth quirked into that crazily attractive smile. 'Oh, you'll be quite safe,' he taunted softly. 'That is, if you're sure you want to be.' He dropped to his haunches in front of her, and as she tried to turn her head away he caught her chin in his hand and compelled her to lift her eyes to meet his. 'If you really don't want me to touch you, little Kate,' he murmured, very low, 'you must stop looking at me like that.'

Her heart was pounding so fast she felt dizzy. His thumb brushed lightly across her trembling lips, and for one wild, wanton moment she was certain that he was going to bring to life all her crazy fantasies. She was defenceless—too naked, too vulnerable. His fingertips slid slowly down her arm, and she felt herself growing weak . . .

But abruptly he turned away, and picked up her T-shirt, thrusting it into her hands with a wry grin. 'Here, put this on and come and give me a hand with the scanner,' he said, his voice as cool as ever.

Awash with emotions she couldn't even begin to unravel, she turned away from him, and pulled the T-shirt on over her head.

'See if there's a small screwdriver under the dashboard, would you?' asked Sean, impersonally polite. Relieved—of course she was relieved—that the dangerous moment of intimacy was past, she scrambled across the helm seat, found a small electrician's screwdriver in the glove compartment, and took it back to him. 'Thanks,' he said briefly, giving her the bigger screwdriver to hold for him.

She watched in fascination as his strong hands worked with deftness and precision over the delicate connections, half afraid that if she let herself look up at him he would be able to read in her eyes the thoughts that were burning in her brain. But though she kept her gaze lowered, she was overpoweringly aware of him, and the desire to touch him was almost out of control.

When he turned to her and said, 'Come here a minute,' she started almost guiltily, her mouth dry. She approached warily, reluctant to stand so close to him. 'Just hold this wire in place for me, while I tighten the screw,' he requested, and she did as he bid, hoping that her hand would not shake too much. 'That's it,' he said at last. 'Just a loose connection. I was afraid I was going to have to take the whole thing to pieces.'

'Do you know how to do that?' she asked, surprised.

He laughed drily. 'Of course I do. I can fix anything on this boat. It's essential when you might be stranded on one of the out-islands, miles from anywhere.'

'Where did you learn it all? she enquired curiously.

'Mostly from my grandfather,' he answered, exchanging screwdrivers with her again.

'Oh. I suppose there aren't many schools out here on the islands.'

He stared at her, his eyes sparkling with laughter like the sun on the sea. 'Of course there are,' he answered, richly amused.

She flushed with embarrassment. 'I'm sorry ... I . . .'

'Did you think I was illiterate, then?' he teased.

'No, but ... I thought you were probably the type to skip school and go fishing,' she stammered.

'Oh, I was,' he admitted cheerfully. 'When I could get away with it. The old man was pretty strict on that—he wanted me to get a college education.'

'You went to college?'

'Uh-huh.' He closed the casing of the radar-scanner, and turned back to her, that quirkily attractive smile curving his mouth. 'Not that I let it interfere with the serious business of fishing, though,' he added.

'No—well, you'd have to keep your priorities right, wouldn't you?' she returned, matching his light tone. 'What did you do at college?'

'Played football and picked up girls,' he told her, wicked humour in his eyes.

'Football?' she queried, deliberately ignoring the second half of his statement. 'Oh, you mean that crazy game like rugby where all the players pad themselves up like Superman and spend all their time in scrums?'

'Yes, that crazy game,' he agreed, grinning. 'And I take leave to inform you, young lady, that you happen to be talking to the second best quarter-back on campus.'

'Only second best?' she teased, her dark eyes slanting up to his, full of mischief.

'The best guy turned pro, and went on to win the Super-Bowl.'

'Oh, well. That would account for it.'

He leaned against the radar-scanner, and surveyed her with a speculative gaze. 'That's better,' he remarked.

She looked up at him questioningly. 'What is?'

'You're flirting with me.'

A swift blush rose to her cheeks. 'I am not,' she protested, all too aware that her trembling voice betrayed her tension.

He laughed softly. 'Yes you are,' he insisted, his voice taking on a note of husky intimacy. 'You're good at it, too. You should do it more often.'

Caught off-guard, she took swift refuge behind a makeshift defence. 'You seem to forget that I recently lost my husband,' she countered in glacial tones.

'Oh, I haven't forgotten,' he answered, untroubled by her anger. 'But that was a year ago, Kate. You can't go on mourning for ever.'

'And what gives you the right to tell me when I should stop?' she flashed bitterly.

He sighed in exasperation. 'Okay, I don't have any right at all. But don't you see that you're throwing your life away, clinging to the past like this?'

'Just because I don't want to be one of your one-night stands,' she threw at him in reckless fury.

He caught her arm as she tried to step past him, and his eyes taunted her. 'Don't you?' he murmured provocatively. 'Maybe you should try it. It might be just what you need.'

'Take your hands off me!' she hissed fiercely. 'I don't need your kind of therapy. You're nothing but a . . . a reprobate.'

He burst out laughing. 'Well, I've been called a few things in my time,' he taunted, 'but that's a new one.'

'I can think of a few more,' she told him in a voice that would strip paint, 'but I'm too much of a lady to repeat them.'

His lip curled cynically as he released his hold on her arm. 'Oh, you're a lady all right,' he sneered. 'But don't give yourself airs, little Kate. Ladies like you, or tarts like Maxie—in my bed, you're all the same.'

Her palm itched to slap his arrogant face, but she sensed that he was waiting for her to try. So with a flounce of frustrated rage she turned away from him, and hurried down the ladder to the safe haven of her own cabin, where she threw herself on to the bunk, a trembling bundle of overstretched nerves.

It was some time before Kate felt sufficiently

composed to venture from her cabin. Eventually, refreshed by a warm shower and dressed in jeans and a white sweater, she went back up to the saloon. She picked up her book, and settled down to read, trying to ignore Sean.

He was standing on the aft-deck, his hands loosely in the pockets of his jeans, staring out across the open water, breathing deeply the soft evening air. The sun was setting, tingeing the banking clouds in delicate shades of pink and mauve, deepening to a dramatic indigo as night swept in from the eastern horizon.

Josh came up from the galley to serve dinner. 'English chow tonight,' he announced proudly. 'Fish 'n' chips.'

But when she saw what he had set out on the table on the aft-deck, she laughed. 'I doubt if many English fish 'n' chip shops serve shark cutlets,' she told him.

'They don't know what they're missing,' remarked Sean. 'It's very good.'

It was, too—tender and succulent, served with crisp golden chips and creamy sweetcorn, laced with the inevitable peppers.

But Kate was on edge throughout the meal. She knew that somehow she had to try to re-establish the idea of a business relationship between them. She didn't want him to think that what had happened up on the flying-bridge had upset her unduly. She had just been a little ... startled by his sudden appearance, that was all. After all, she had sunbathed topless in the South of France with Dave and thought nothing of it. It was a little different, here in the close environment of the boat, of course, and she wouldn't do it again.

'You were right. That was delicious. Josh is a very good cook,' she remarked, hoping her voice didn't betray her tension. 'Has he worked for you long?'

'He's been sailing with me since he was knee-high,' Sean answered, relaxing back lazily in his seat. 'His grandfather worked for mine.'

'Really?' asked Kate with polite interest. 'Was your grandfather a shark-hunter too?'

Sean laughed softly. 'No. He was a blockade-runner.'

Kate choked over her coffee. 'What?'

'Prohibition,' he explained in a matter-of-fact tone. 'He used to run illegal liquor out of Mexico up to Florida.' Kate stared at him, not sure if he was joking. 'You don't believe me?' he teased. 'It was rife in the islands, right up to the repeal of the Volstead Act in 1933. Some of the best families were involved. There was a great deal of money in it.'

Kate eyed him sceptically. 'Did your grandfather make a lot of money?' she enquired.

'He did quite well.'

'And yet you choose to live above that awful bar where I met you?' she demanded, unable to keep the scorn from her voice.

He laughed again, faintly mocking. 'I own it,' he told her. 'You seem shocked.'

'Well, it isn't exactly ... I mean ...' Her voice trailed away uncertainly.

'It's a dive,' he agreed readily. 'So what? Sailors on shore leave want a good drink at an honest price, not lace curtains and gentility.'

Kate's cheeks flushed scarlet. 'It's the most horrible place I've ever been into in my life,' she declared, remembering all those hungry stares.

His eyes glinted, taunting her. 'So I should hope,' he remarked. 'It isn't at all the sort of place a respectable young lady should visit.'

'So why do you live there?' she challenged.

'I like it. It's very convenient, right in the middle of town.'

'Yes, but . . .' Her gaze shifted uncomfortably as she remembered Maxie, with her scarlet lips and breakneck curves.

'But you don't think much of the company I keep?' he enquired with unnerving perceptiveness. 'At least I know that if anyone is going to stick a knife in my back, it'll be the sort I can see.'

Kate blinked at him in astonishment. His hard mouth had curled into something close to a sneer. 'Such innocent eyes, little Kate,' he murmured mockingly. 'It's hard to believe that you were married to Dave Taylor.'

'What do you mean?' she demanded, startled.

He leaned towards her, and she felt herself trembling like a trapped butterfly. 'How long were you married before he died?' he asked, his voice soft but strangely compelling.

'Four months,' she told him, wishing that she could have told him instead to mind his own business.

'Ah, maybe that explains it,' he mused.

'What do you mean?' she repeated, tears springing to her eyes.

'You never really had time to get to know him, did you?' he asked quietly.

'I knew him well enough,' she retorted, her voice breaking. 'Well enough to know that I loved him, and I always will. No one else will ever take his place.' She stumbled blindly to her feet. 'Excuse me,' she mumbled, hardly even knowing what she was saying. 'I'm rather tired. It must be all the fresh air. I think I'll have an early night.'

She escaped down the steps to her cabin and closed the door behind here quickly, leaning against it, shaking from head to foot. His strange words were spinning in her brain. What on earth had he meant? Why should he dislike Dave so much, when by his own admission he had known him only a little, a long time ago?

She sat down on the bunk and picked up the silver-framed photograph of Dave, and stared into those smiling eyes, as if seeking an answer to the riddle. But she found no enlightenment, only more questions. Why had Dave never mentioned Sean's name? What had been at the root of their quarrel? Rivalry? Money? A woman?

Suddenly it seemed that the dangers down on the reef could be the least that she faced on this trip. A malicious twist of fate had placed her in the hands of a man who harboured a long-standing grudge against her husband. It had begun to seem as though that treacherous tug of attraction she felt towards Sean was even worse than unfaithfulness to Dave. It was a betrayal.

With a sigh she put the photo down, and began to get ready for bed. Putting on the dainty, pale pink cotton Japanese-style pyjamas she liked to wear, she climbed into her bunk and drew the quilt up around her. She read for a little while, trying to distract her mind from her present difficulties.

Before she switched off the light, she whispered a sad good night to the picture of Dave, as she always did. But when at last she drifted into the uncharted territory of dreams it was to find that Sean's marauding presence had slipped past her guard.

The tension tingled in the air like lightning the following morning. The few words that Kate spoke to Sean were stilted, and she received only cool monosyllables in return. She felt a little sorry for young Josh, who sensed the hostility and looked from one to the other like a bewildered puppy.

Kate almost wanted to pretend that she felt too tired, and didn't want to dive—she felt to raw too face the closeness they always seemed to share beneath the water, knowing that once the dive was over everything would return again to this rather uncomfortable normality.

But as the position of the sun and a glance at her watch told her that it was a little after ten o'clock she remarked as evenly as she could, 'It's time to get suited-up.'

'Uh-huh,' grunted Sean, not looking up from the magazine he was reading.

She threw him a frosty glare, but it was wasted on his stony profile. Quelling the urge to shout at him just to startle him out of his infuriating implacability, she went down to her cabin to change into her swimsuit. When she climbed back up on deck, Sean was already in his wetsuit and was checking the diving-gear.

Kate donned her wetsuit in silence, and it wasn't until they were down on the swim platform that Sean spoke. 'Are you ready?' he asked.

'Just about.'

'Right. We should be able to get finished on this reef today. I'm afraid it looks as if we've drawn a blank again.' His tone wasn't quite friendly, but at least it was a little less remote.

'Oh, well,' she sighed resignedly. 'If at first you don't succeed . . . Come on, then. let's eliminate this one, and then we can see where we want to go next.'

She let go of the ladder, and rolled into the neat somersault that would take her clear of the boat. As always she felt that peculiar little thrill of excitement at the prospect of a dive, a kind of heightened awareness that honed all her senses. The metallic sounds from the boat and their own breathing-apparatus sang like some weird, surreal orchestra; the sunlight filtered down in sapphire shafts as if into some vast cathedral. Her very skin seemed to pick up signals from the water, eddying currents and the disparate movements of fish, drawing a kind of map for her.

How she envied the fish, with their freedom to move around in this underwater world, unhindered by the need to carry their own air-supply. She had heard tales of divers who had gone down to those dangerous depths where nitrogen narcosis could produce that strange phenomenon, poetically called 'rapture of the deeps'. Even the most rational and experienced of divers could go slightly crazy, and some had been known to take off their air-tanks and throw them away.

But at a mere fifty feet there was no danger of experiencing such bizarre effects—though a lapse of concentration could be equally dangerous, she warned herself sternly, bringing her mind back to the job in hand.

Their search along the outer arm of the reef seemed doomed to failure yet again. There was just once more stand of coral to investigate—a forlorn hope, if she was honest. She checked her watch—they still had eight minutes left, longer if they decided to make this their only dive of the day.

She borrowed Sean's diving-knife—the blade was longer and thicker than her own—to prise up a growth of silvery star-coral. It was firmly anchored to whatever was beneath it, and the weightlessness of her body in the water made it difficult to exert much force.

Sean tried, as she glanced around to check that the sea was safe. Everything seemed normal, and she turned back to Sean . . . and then at the same moment they both seemed to sense something, and turned round again. There was nothing—too much nothing. The shoals of fish that had been skittering around them had vanished.

And then with a chill of horror Kate realised what the slow, steady thudding in the water was—shark. Even as the thought crystallised in her mind, an evil shape emerged from the blue-green fog along the reef.

Instinctively she reached out her hand for Sean, and felt the reassuring brush of his fingers as he carefully manoeuvred her behind him. She gripped his weight-belt with one hand, easing her diving-knife from the holster strapped around her leg, and backed slowly towards the reef, making no sudden movements.

It was a white-tipped reef-shark, not large as sharks go but not noted for its friendliness. The fish came close—so close that every murderous detail was clear—the black, staring eye, the vicious slash of a mouth, filled with razor-sharp teeth. Closer, until she felt as if she could reach out and touch the pale, abrasive skin.

Its body was sleek and beautiful, so perfectly adapted to its environment that it had remained unchanged since the age of the dinosaurs, long before the first mammal ancestors of man had even begun to evolve. All those millions of years. It was an awesome thought.

The fish slid silently past them, the powerful undulations of its caudal fin propelling it in a smooth, deadly glide. Kate gripped Sean's belt, fighting to hold her terror in check as the fish turned and came back. 'Kill it' she wanted to scream—but she knew that Sean would never risk putting blood in the water unless he had no alternatives left. If there were more sharks in the vicinity, it could attract them to a feeding frenzy.

The fish passed them by again, closer still. It seemed to be sniffing at them, not sure if it fancied this strange, rubbery creature that had invaded its world. Kate had heard that sharks didn't like the smell of wetsuits. 'Go away,' she tried to transmit into that dull fish-brain. 'You don't want to eat us. We don't taste very nice.' She realised that she was very close to hysteria. They were trapped against the reef, and their air was running out.

It was over in seconds. Without warning the fish turned, and flashed towards them, and the next instant it was twisting away, blood streaming from a wound in its head. But there was only one cartridge in the shark-stick. Before Kate even had time to realise what was happening, Sean had gripped her firmly around the waist and was towing her swiftly through the water towards the shark-cage. Behind them the water was boiling, but she didn't look back.

Sean bundled her unceremoniously into the shark-cage and swam in behind her, closing the door. She turned instinctively in his arms, and buried her face against his broad chest. The jerky pull on the cage told her that Josh was winding them to the surface. It seemed to take an eternity, though in reality it was barely a minute, before they broke the surface, and she fumbled to remove her mouth-piece so that she could savour the sweet taste of fresh, natural air.

Sean lifted her out of the shark-cage as if she were a rag doll. She clung to him weakly, her legs buckling beneath her, and he cursed softly as he stripped off her face-mask and her air-tanks. He unzipped the heavy neoprene suit, helped her out of it gently, and wrapped her up in a cocoon of big, fluffy towel.

She hadn't realised she was crying until she felt him kiss away the tears from the corners of her eyes, but then her mouth sought instinctively for his, her lips parting hungrily as he responded to her silent plea. Swirling heat invaded her trembling body, blotting out the horror of the crazed fish with a new and exquisite sensation that spun her out of control.

All the painful desire that had racked her body for the past few weeks surfaced irresistibly, and communicated itself with wanton clarity to the man who was holding her so tightly. She felt the hardness of his body against hers, felt the vibrant tension of male arousal in him, and she curved herself towards him in willing surrender.

He lifted his head, and looked down into her upturned face, laughing as if bemused by her unexpected response. 'Hey,' he murmured smokily, 'if this is what happens when you get a bit of a fright . . .'

Her cheeks flamed scarlet as realisation flooded into her mind, and she struggled violently out of his arms. 'Let me go,' she spat at him, her anger as hot as only seconds before had been her desire. He released her at once, and she backed away nervously, snatching at the trailing corner of the towel. 'How *dare* you touch me?' she uttered furiously.

He laughed. 'You're one crazy lady,' he declared, shaking his head, 'I've got no more idea what's going on in that mixed-up brain of yours than if you were one of those damned fish!'

'Maybe I just don't like the bait you're offering,' she jibed.

His eyes flashed with anger. 'Maybe you just haven't tasted enough of it yet,' he countered swiftly, moving towards her. She turned to run, but the towel tripped her and he caught her quickly, turning her in his arms and lifting her almost off her feet.

She fought wildly to escape, but he was far too strong for her. His fingers curled in her wet hair, dragging her head back painfully, warning her not to resist further. As his mouth touched hers she stilled, determined to remain cold and passive. She felt the languorous sweep of his sensuous tongue over the delicate inner softness of her lips, but still she clenched her teeth against him in defiance, until another punishing tug on her hair forced her to yield.

Then began an invasion that ravaged her mouth with a fierce demand against which there was no defence. His hard hands curved her body intimately against his, reminding her all too clearly of the danger she had so recklessly courted.

She acknowledged his mastery while stubbornly refusing to admit any pleasure in it. But she was weakening, her body was responding treacherously, her will imprisoned. And then as if he sensed the moment at which she conceded defeat he put her away from him, his eyes burning but his voice harshly mocking.

'There. Let that be a lesson to you,' he warned roughly. 'Don't start something you haven't got the guts to finish.'

'I hate you,' she snarled at him, her body trembling with reaction. 'Don't ever touch me again. I'll kill you.'

He laughed in cynical amusement. 'Don't tempt me, little Kate,' he taunted her, 'that sure would be one hell of a way to go!'

She stumbled blindly down to her cabin and, stripping of the silky-thin swimsuit, plunged into the shower, letting the soothing warm water run down over her flaming skin, melting with the salt tears that streamed from her eyes.

In just those few moments up on deck, Sean McGregor had finally shattered the brittle shell with which she had surrounded herself, leaving her vulnerable—more vulnerable than she had ever been. Before Dave, she had had one or two boyfriends, lads of her own age, as inexperienced as she was herself. They had progressed no further than a few clumsy kisses. And even with Dave, before their marriage, her body had been unawakened. It had been quite easy to keep things under control.

But she had never known such a scorching swirl of sensation, even with Dave, as she had felt in Sean's arms. That realisation shocked her. She had never thought she could feel such a searing response to a man she barely knew, didn't even like. It was a primeval thing, frightening—far more frightening than the sharks.

Maybe . . . maybe it had been only reaction, after all—reaction to the terror of the sharks; relief, perhaps, and gratitude to him for rescuing her. But the prickly honesty of her mind would not let her hide behind that convenient excuse.

No—Sean McGregor held a power over her, try as she might to evade it. Tears of humiliation stung her eyes. How could she defend herself against him, when her own wild desires betrayed her so easily? But defend herself she must. He was a ruthless opponent, and in victory would leave her nothing—not even her self-respect.

A grim suspicion was gnawing at the back of her mind. Could he be just using her as a pawn, to win some kind of bitter revenge against Dave? She shook her head impatiently. She was just being foolish. The long hours of boredom were causing her imagination to run riot.

Nevertheless, she must be careful to avoid another scene like that one. With that thought held firmly in her mind, she turned off the water and stepped out of the shower. Ten minutes later, dressed in shorts and a T-shirt, her hair already drying into clustering curls around her head, she went back upstairs.

'You didn't drink your chocolate after your dive, Miz Kate,' Josh reminded her with his usual beaming smile. 'You want it now?'

'No, thanks, Josh. I wouldn't mind a coffee, though, if it's not too much trouble.' She glanced at him cautiously, her cheeks faintly pink. She was sure he had not actually been on deck during her embarrassing scene with Sean, but she wondered uneasily how much of it he and his father had witnessed from the saloon.

She settled herself on the aft-deck, her feet tucked up beneath her, and began to write up her log-book, sipping the coffee that Josh had brought her. But inside she was quivering with tension as she waited for Sean to reappear.

But when at last he came out on deck his manner was as relaxed as if nothing had happened. Kate envied him his ability to be so cool—it was as if he had never kissed her.

'We might as well leave this reef to the sharks,' he said. 'I thought we'd take a break for a couple of days, run down to one of the out-islands.'

'That sounds like a good idea,' she answered, her voice only a little unsteady. 'Where are we going to go?'

'There's a place called Wrecker's Cay. It'll only take us a couple of hours to get there. We can dine ashore this evening if you like. There's a hotel that does a decent meal.'

'That would be nice,' Kate agreed. 'How did it get the name Wrecker's Cay?' she added curiously, relieved that she could still manage to hold a normal conversation with him after all that had happened.

He sat down on the bench-seat opposite her, stretching his long legs across the deck. 'There's a sandbank running out from it, very treacherous to shipping,' he told her. 'In the old days a lot of ships ran aground on it. The islanders used to plunder them for their cargo. You can still see the skeletons of some of them, encrusted in the coral, though most of them were burned, or towed off at high water to be scuttled well away from the island.'

'What happened to the crews?'

He drew a finger across his throat.

Kate shuddered. 'How bloodthirsty! It seems strange to think that such a lovely part of the world as this should have seen so much violence and murder.'

'You'll have to meet my grandfather,' remarked Sean. 'He could tell you tales that would curl your liver!'

'I'd love to,' she agreed eagerly. 'What's the hotel like? Should I wear a dress?'

'If you like, though a lot of people don't bother—the out-islands are pretty informal.'

'Oh, it'll make a change to get out of jeans,' she said. 'I think I'll go and get ready.'

CHAPTER FIVE

THE sun was setting as they approached Wrecker's Cay, painting the sky with wispy streaks of lavender and mauve. Kate had almost forgotten her reservations about Sean in the anticipation of going ashore. It was fun to have the opportunity of putting on her best dress, and making herself look pretty with make-up.

When she was ready, she surveyed her reflection critically. Her hair was a little too short for sophistication, but the halo of dark curls suited her fine-boned face. Her skin glowed with a honey-gold sheen, and her dark eyes were fringed by long silky lashes that needed no mascara. But she had added a touch of pearly shadow to define their almond shape, and had slicked a shimmer of glowing colour over her lips.

The dress seduced by subtle definition of her curves, and swirled around her feet as she moved. She knew that she was not a classical beauty, even by generous standards, but she had a certain feminine allure that might startle Sean a little after days of seeing her in tomboyish clothes. A small smile curved her delicate mouth as she stepped up into the saloon.

The effect was everything she had hoped for. Sean was talking to Josh, his back to her; as the younger man's eyes widened in surprise he turned—and banged his head against the deck-head beam that he usually so automatically avoided. Kate gurgled with laughter.

'Well,' he protested, rubbing his forehead ruefully, 'if you're going to suddenly turn up looking like that, you ought to send out advance warning.'

'Is that a compliment?' she asked demurely.

'You bet it is.'

She lowered her eyes quickly, unable to sustain the note of light flirtation. 'Thank you,' she murmured. 'Is it time to go?'

'We might as well,' answered Sean. "Bye, Josh. Have a nice weekend. See you on Monday.'

'Are you planning to spend the weekend at the hotel then?' Kate asked as Sean handed her across the short gangway to the wooden quayside.

'No. Josh and his father are going to visit their family for a couple of days,' he told her.

'Oh.' She slanted him a glance of sharp suspicion. Why had he not told her that they would be spending the whole weekend alone on the boat? But after all, they would be in port. If he became difficult, she could always take a room ashore.

She drew her fine silk wrap closer round her shoulders, too aware of that compelling maleness that he exuded, apparently unconsciously. He was dressed with casual stylishness in dark slacks and a well-cut, cream-coloured jacket, his cream shirt open at the throat, and he walked with long, lazy strides like a wolf on the Steppes.

A neat gravel path led through a garden, beneath tall jacarandas, decked with hibiscus and oleander that by day would be a riot of colour. Light spilled from lamps set low among the flowerbeds, and Kate realised that the odd electric whirring they seemed to make was caused by giant moths, held captive by the hypnotic beams.

They rounded a low hump of land that separated the yacht marina from the hotel, and Kate paused, her eyes widening in astonishment. The hotel was much larger than she had expected, startlingly modern, almost surreal in the clear night air. It was long and low, a honeycomb of bronzed glass and white concrete, aflame with lights. A wide, flower-decked terrace separated it from a sweep of palm-shaded beach.

'Very smart,' accorded Kate wryly, glad she had chosen to dress up a little.

'I'm glad you like it,' Sean answered, a hint of dryness in his voice.

'I didn't say I liked it,' she corrected him. 'I just said it was smart. I dare say it's stacked to the rafters with millionares.'

'You have some objection to millionaires?'

She shrugged her shoulders to indicate her indifference. 'I suppose some of them are probably nice enough as individuals,' she answered doubtfully.

'What an odd prejudice,' he remarked. 'Most young women can hardly be restrained from falling at their feet.'

'More fool them,' she concluded dismissively.

He laughed, not his usual cynical laugh, but a laugh of genuine amusement. 'Shall we dine there anyway?' he suggested.

'Don't you have to book a table in advance?' she enquired, reluctant to let him buy her what was certainly going to be a very expensive meal, but unsure of his reaction if she insisted on paying for herself.

'I radioed in to let them know we were coming,' he explained.

'Oh.' She could think of nothing else to say. They walked on down the path, and in through the wide glass doors to the foyer of the hotel.

'Good evening, Mr McGregor.'

'Evening, Lucas. Busy tonight?'

Kate glanced in surprise at the immaculately-dressed desk-clerk who had greeted Sean with such deference.

'Quite full, sir,' he told Sean with satisfaction. 'Good evening, Mrs Taylor,' he added with a polite little bow.

'Good evening,' she stammered in uncertain response, allowing Sean to lead her into the large, softly lit dining-room. The tables were set around a small square of gleaming parquet, where a few couples danced to the music of a brightly dressed band playing the local lilting goombay music. Sean led her straight to one of the best tables, and flipped over a reserved sign.

'You must be a very important customer,' she commented drily as he offered her a seat.

'There are one or two things . . .'

'Sean! What a pleasant surprise!'

An unmistakable frown flickered across Sean's face, but as he turned his voice was pleasant enough. 'Hello, there, Serge,' he said. 'May I introduce Kate Taylor? Kate—Serge François.'

A gleaming smile flashed from a darkly handsome Latin face that was not quite so familiar to Kate as the name. 'Welcome to Wrecker's Cay, Miss Taylor,' he purred, bowing over her hand with extravagant gallantry. Her mother would be swooning, she reflected wryly—Serge François was one of her favourite singers. His warm brown eyes moved in swift, approving survey of her slender figure, and returned to gaze with consciously exerted magnetism into hers. 'How long do you stay?'

'Just the weekend,' she answered breezily, amused by the fleeting uncertainly in his eyes as he sensed that his charm had not quite swept her off her feet.

He recovered swiftly. 'Ah, then we must persuade Sean to stay a little longer, yes?' he suggested, not releasing her hand as he turned enquiringly to Sean.

'How long we stay is entirely for *Mrs* Taylor to decide,' Sean responded drily. 'She has chartered the *Barracuda*.'

'Chartered?' His expressive face registered surprised query.

'I'm hunting for a wreck,' she explained briefly, 'An old pirate ship.'

'Ah!' Uninvited, he twisted a chair round from an adjacent table, and sat down. 'But that is fascinating,' he declared, gazing earnestly into her eyes. 'Tell me all about it.'

'Shall we order first?' interrupted Sean, the faint gleam of amusement in his eyes telling her that he had sensed that she was not much impressed by Serge's flattery.

Piqued, she turned to Serge the brilliance of her smile. 'There's so much to choose from,' she sighed, her eyes flirting with him over the menu. 'What do you recommend?'

'But you must try the crawfish,' he insisted warmly. 'It has but lately returned to the tables—there is a closed season, you see.'

'Very well, the crawfish,' she agreed at once.

'And meanwhile,' he went on smoothly, 'may I have the pleasure of a dance?'

'I'd love to.' She resisted the temptation to glance back at Sean in triumph as she placed her hand in Serge's and let him lead her out on to the floor. He encircled her with his arms, and she put her hand against his chest to keep a little distance between them as she caught a whiff of his slightly cloying cologne.

'You have known Sean long?' he enquired politely.

'No,' she answered. 'I chartered the *Barracuda* in Nassau two weeks ago. I hadn't met him before. He was . . . an acquaintance of my husband.'

'Really?' Serge laughed softly. 'I wonder when Sean went into the charter business?' he mused.

Kate stared up at him in amazement. 'But I thought . . . I thought that was his business?' she queried, her brows drawn together in confusion.

'But no, *ma chérie*. Did he not tell you?' He drew her closer as he wove expertly among the dancers. 'He is the grandson of Nathan McGregor.' The name meant nothing to Kate, until he added, 'He owns this hotel.'

She gasped, and looked round quickly at their table, but it was empty. She sought among the dancers, and found him at once, taller than those around him, his sun-bleached hair gleaming in the pinpoints of light circling the dance-floor. He was dancing with a fluttery blonde in a vivid cerise dress, and laughing at something she was saying.

Serge's glance followed hers. 'Ah, I see Sean has wasted no time in renewing his aquaintance with the lovely Georgina,' he remarked, an edge of sarcasm in his voice. 'He knows well how to entertain himself, *n'est-ce pas?*'

'She's very pretty,' agreed Kate in a strained voice.

Serge lifted his shoulders in a dismissive shrug. 'She is a charming piece of fluff,' he remarked disparagingly, gazing down at Kate with warm eyes as if to convey that he found her far more fascinating. 'But of course, that is exactly to Sean's taste,' he added with nice disdain. 'I hear that the young lady he keeps in Nassau is similarly generous with her favours.'

Kate stiffened, and he looked down at her quickly. 'I hope I have not offended?' he begged earnestly. 'I understood . . .?' He left the sentence hanging questioningly.

'Not at all,' Kate responded, her jaw aching with the effort of smiling. 'Mr McGregor's private life has nothing whatsoever to do with me. Our relationship is strictly business.'

He smiled slowly, caressingly. 'Ah, that is good,' he murmured, trying to draw her even closer into his arms. 'I had guessed that it must be so. It is evident that you are not at all the type that my friend Sean is lamentably inclined to pursue. And of course, he never dallies with married women. He is, in his way, quite old-fashioned.'

His tone implied that he was hampered by no such quaint inhibitions, and Kate drew away from him, her eyes cold. 'Do we have to keep talking about Sean?' she asked tautly.

'Many apologies,' he purred, satisfied that he had defamed his rival enough. 'Alas, I fear the waiter is ready to serve you, and so I must let you go—at least for the present.' He conveyed her back to their table, bowing over her hand as Sean approached. 'I may hope to see you again while you are here?'

She bestowed on him her most charming smile, hoping Sean would notice. 'Of course,' she agreed, letting her voice take on a slightly husky timbre. 'I would like that very much.'

He kissed the tips of her fingers, and withdrew, his smile triumphant as he exchanged a few brief words with Sean.

But the cynical amusement in Sean's blue eyes as he took his seat across the table told her that he was in no danger of succumbing to jealousy. 'Wine?' he asked, filling her glass without waiting for a reply.

'Thank you.'

'Be careful of Serge,' he advised her, his voice expressionless. 'That Gallic charm can turn on and off like a tap.'

'Thank you for the warning,' she returned, an inflexion of ironic humour in her voice. 'Rather a case of the pot calling the kettle black, don't you think?' He acknowledged the jibe with a sardonic smile. 'As a matter of fact, we were talking about you,' she went on boldly. 'I understand now why we had no trouble getting a table.'

He sat back in his seat, sipping his wine, that mocking smile still curving his hard mouth. 'I was going to tell you about that, before Serge's unwelcome intervention.'

'Why didn't you tell me before?'

He shrugged his wide shoulders in cool indifference. 'It didn't seem relevant to our business relationship,' he drawled laconically.

Kate was spared the need to reply at once by the arrival of the waiter with their first course. Then she asked levelly, 'Does your grandfather own only this hotel, or is there a chain of them across the western hemisphere?'

'He owns half a dozen,' he answered disinterestedly.

'Really? And I suppose you'll inherit the lot?' she persisted, her voice dripping sarcasm.

'Eventually.' His eyes warned her to stop trying to bait him, and she fell silent, concentrating on her meal, which was excellent. So too was the wine, though she was no expert: mellow and golden, with a flavour so perfectly balanced that at first she had not fully appreciated its quality. But now she was noting the deep, satisfying undertones, so different from the cheap, light wines she was used to—swift to please, but sometimes a little disappointing in aftertaste.

The dance-band had left the stage, and into the single spotlight stepped Serge, resplendent now in a black velvet suit and and white shirt that foamed with lace at the throat. He sang several romantic ballads, in that honey-smooth voice, strolling among the tables, a red rose in his hand. Every woman he passed, from eighteen to eighty, he favoured with a little intimate flattery, and their eyes glowed as they watched him move on round the room. At last, crooning words of love, he came to Kate, and with a final eloquent flourish offered her the rose.

She took it with a slight smile, uncomfortable in the spotlight. He finished the song, and turned to milk the applause, leaving her in blessed darkness again. She was aware of Sean watching her across the table, making it difficult to maintain her composure.

The image she had built of him had been fragmented by the events of the day—the gentleness and savagery of his kiss, and then the startling discovery that his life was not what he had led her to believe. Her eyes travelled around the luxurious dining-room—heavens, he must be the heir to a multi-million dollar fortune! He could have any woman he wanted! And yet he chose to live above that sleazy bar in Nassau, and to chase light-skirted women like Maxie and Georgina.

Covertly she watched him, trying to put together the jigsaw pieces that kept eluding her. Why had he turned his back on the kind of society to which his fortune would have given him automatic *entrée*? Into her mind came the words he had spoken, that evening at dinner: 'At least if someone is going to stick a knife in my back, it'll be the sort I can see.' Someone . . . Who? Dave? Surely not . . .

'What's wrong?' She glanced up questioningly as

Sean's words cut across her train of thought. 'You were frowning.'

She smiled brightly across the table. 'Was I? Oh, I was just . . . hoping you weren't going to ask me to go Dutch,' she temporised quickly.

'I wouldn't dream of it. More wine? Or would you prefer coffee?'

'Coffee, please.' He caught the waiter's eye, and ordered the coffee. Kate twiddled absently with the corner of her napkin, trying to sort out the turmoil in her mind. 'Why did you let me think you were in the charter business?' she burst out.

'I was afraid of what you might do if I refused to help you find this damn wreck of yours,' he responded. 'You seemed a little hot-headed.'

'I could have managed without you,' she declared, her eyes flashing defiance. 'It might have taken me a little longer, that's all.'

'You could have spent the rest of your life searching among those reefs.'

'If that's how long it takes, that's fine by me,' she retorted, her eyes glittering.

'And how would you support yourself?' he enquired sardonically. 'There isn't much call for English school teachers around here.'

'I'd find another sort of job,' she insisted obstinately.

'Doing what?' he mocked. 'What else are you trained for? Pulling pints in a place like the Runner?'

'I wouldn't work there if I was starving!'

Sean laughed softly. 'I don't think I'd hire you,' he drawled. 'I don't think you'd be up to it.' Their eyes met in brief conflict, and then Sean rose to his feet, his mouth quirking into that devastatingly attractive smile. 'But since the problem doesn't arise,' he added, 'let's dance, and forget all these quarrels for a while, shall we?'

He took her hand before she could pull it away, and drew her to her feet and into his arms, and they moved out on to the dance-floor. The band had returned to the stage, and their lilting music swayed with the slow, compulsive rhythm of the sea. He overcame her instinctive recoil, holding her far too close for modesty, and she had to submit or risk making an embarrassing scene.

So she let him hold her, let him move her to the music; and slowly, imperceptibly, the male muskiness of his body invaded her senses, the warm strength of his arms melted the steel in her spine. He danced well, and Kate knew that every female in the place was watching her with envy—and her mouth curved in a secret smile of satisfaction.

The music changed, and the band began to play a rock and roll medley. Sean took her hands, and began to jive with her, spinning and catching her with faultless timing. The lively dancing exhilarated her, making her eyes glow and her pulse beat faster, and she smiled up into Sean's eyes, all hostility forgotten.

When the beat slowed again, she let him draw her back into his arms without resistance. She rested her cheek against his chest, and felt his breath warm in her hair. She closed her eyes, and slowly the whole world faded away, until it seemed as though there were no reality beyond the circle of his arms. A deep, feminine submissiveness flowed through her; she had forgotten her defences, and they were crumbling behind her as she danced.

One melody drifted into another, and she had no thought of time—she could have rested there for all eternity. When at last Sean said softly, 'I think we'd better call it a night now, Kate. The band want to go to bed,' she opened her eyes to realise with a stab of shock and embarrassment that the place was virtually deserted except for a few waiters quietly clearing the tables.

'Oh!' she gasped, and drew away from him. The band leader grinned at her, clapping his hands in ironic applause. Her face flushed scarlet, and she searched in bewilderment for their table, where she had left her things. Sean was there before her, putting her bag into her hands and wrapping her silk shawl around her shoulders.

The brush of his fingers was strangely electric, and she kept her eyes lowered, aware that the last hour or more spent dancing in his arms had once more edged their relationship towards an intimacy that she didn't want to consider. She had meant to keep him at a cool distance this evening, but she knew that she had lost control of the whole thing. One minute she was snarling at him, the next smiling. He was playing with her, as he would play with a shark on his line, luring her on to his bait, letting her exhaust herself with struggling until he could take her whenever he wanted her . . .

She shivered with shock at her own train of thought. She was walking beside him, back through the hotel gardens towards the yacht marina. The water was a swathe of velvety-black beneath a sky that was spangled with a million stars. The crescent of the waxing moon rode majestically, high above the horizon. Only a distant glow, far out across the dark water, betrayed the existence of other islands. They could have been adrift in space.

But the tranquil beauty of the scenery could not calm the storm of emotion raging inside her, nor dim her acute awareness of Sean walking along beside her. The sweet, heady perfume of frangipani filled the air, the sea whispered lullabies to the soft coral sand. There was romance in the night, only to be resisted by those of strong will—and Kate knew that her will had been weakened by the music and the wine.

She stole a secret glance up at the man beside her. He was strolling along with his hands in his pockets, totally at ease; the strong line of his jaw bespoke a nature that was always in control. Sean McGregor was a man who took what he wanted from life, and left the rest to turn to dust. A shimmer of heat ran through her. Tonight they would be alone on the boat—and the cabin door would be no barrier against his strength.

But no—that was not his style. He was far too proud a man to resort to breaking down doors. It was the invisible barriers that he would assault—and Kate felt herself to be all too vulnerable.

The marina was quiet, the yachts bobbing and swaying on the gentle swell. The *Barracuda* was in darkness. Sean stepped across the transom, and turned to give Kate his hand as she stepped across the short gangway. She hesitated for a second, feeling herself to be on the threshold of something quite beyond her experience. Yet she feared to betray her nervousness, sure that he would exploit it. So she placed her hand reluctantly in his, hoping he wouldn't notice how it trembled.

But as she stepped down on to the deck he did not release his grip on her fingers, and she could not hide the apprehension in the wide, dark eyes she lifted to his. 'I've warned you before about looking at me like that, little Kate,' he murmured, his voice low and husky.

'I . . . I don't know what you mean,' she stammered.

'Don't you? That's very hard to believe. You're no naïve young innocent in spite of those big beautiful eyes. You've been a married woman—you know what you're asking for.'

She tried to draw away from him, but he held her back. 'Frightened, little Kate? But you want me to kiss you.'

'No I don't,' she insisted desperately.

His soft laughter wrapped around her like a velvet cloak, drawing her to him. 'Oh, yes, you do,' he murmured smokily. 'You want me to do more than kiss you.'

She shook her head dumbly, her resolve evaporating in the heat of his gaze.

'Yes,' he whispered urgently.

Still she shook her head, backing away from him. He made no move to stop her as she turned and half-ran to the door of the saloon. She tugged at it, but it would not budge. 'It's locked,' she protested frantically.

'That's right,' he agreed, his tone dry with mockery.

'Please may I have the key?'

He leaned past her, ostentatiously taking care not to touch her, and pressed out a combination-code to release the computerised lock. The door slid open, and she darted inside, trying with little success not to look as if she was running away from him.

He followed her, closing the door behind him, and stood blocking the passageway through the middle of the saloon, effectively barring her retreat to the safety of her own cabin. She stared at him, trembling from head to foot as she read the dark intent in his eyes. He was not going to let her pass.

She sought desperately for something to say to break the tense silence. 'Well, I suppose I should thank you for a very pleasant evening,' she stammered with a nervous laugh.

'I'm glad you enjoyed it,' he responded evenly. 'Even if the place was stacked to the rafters with millionaires.'

'Oh, yes.' She managed a brittle smile. 'I certainly got hold of the wrong end of the stick, didn't I? There I was, thinking you were just a shark-hunter or something, and all the time you're a big-shot hotel owner. Pretty silly of me, wasn't it?'

He smiled slowly, knowingly. He was winning, without having to move a muscle.

'Why did you let me make such a fool of myself?' she demanded, her voice beginning to rise hysterically. 'I suppose it must have been pretty amusing, eh? Well, I don't think much of your games. They aren't very funny.'

'Would it have made any difference?' he enquired.

'No, of course it wouldn't,' she protested hotly. 'Just because you've got a few noughts on your bank account, it doesn't make me like you any better.'

'That's what I thought,' he responded, his blue eyes gleaming satanically. 'With most girls it can't fail. One whiff of money and they're on the mattress before I even have time to ask their names.'

'How dull it must be,' she spat sarcastically.

'Oh, it is,' he agreed cordially.

Kate glared at him furiously, maddened by his cool self-assurance. Her defences were in ruins, her blood was coursing too quickly in her veins. She had to get away from him, or she would be lost. 'Your love life isn't a subject I wish to discuss,' she said with as much composure as she could muster. 'I think I'll go to bed now.'

His cruel, sensual mouth curved into a smile of evil

mockery. 'I had much the same idea,' he suggested softly.

Her cheeks were flaming. 'I mean my own bed,' she insisted, her voice quavering as her heart raced out of control. 'Alone.'

'Then you'd better come past me,' he challenged, making no move to stand aside.

CHAPTER SIX

HER pulse was beating so fast she felt faint. He was weaving a spell around her, luring her to her destruction with a hypnotic power she couldn't comprehend, couldn't fight. His eyes drew her towards him. Her fingertips longed to feel the warmth of his male flesh, her mouth hungered for the taste of his.

She had forgotten everything—everything but the way he had kissed her hours before, the way his strong arms had held her as they danced. Drawn by that magnetic spell, she reached out a trembling hand to touch the rasp of his cheek, the hard line of his jaw.

Still holding her eyes with that mesmerising gaze, he turned his head and kissed the tips of her fingers, and then swiftly, teasingly, caught them between his strong white teeth, holding them hostage, threatening to bite them off unless she surrendered. She moved closer, and his hands slid round her waist. She was his prisoner, and she knew that she would not be able to escape until he chose to let her go.

His teeth freed her captive fingers as he drew her against him, and her head tipped back as she stared up into his smoky blue eyes. She put her hands up against his powerful shoulders, and her gaze moved down over the hard planes of his face, to rest hungrily on the firm, tempting lines of his mouth, curved still in that slightly mocking smile, taunting her courage to finish what she had started.

Shyly, tentatively, she stretched up on tiptoe, and brushed her lips across his, feeling the tingle as of a thousand electric shocks running through every nerve fibre. She knew that he was deliberately holding back, tormenting her, and she played the moist tip of her tongue into the corners of his lips, entreating a response.

Her heart was racing with fierce excitement, urging her on to defy the danger. He was luring her out of her depth, tricking her into abandoning her defences by making it seem as though it were she seducing him. But she had gone too far, and she didn't know the way back.

When at last he swept her up, ravaging her mouth with savage tenderness, he met not even a feint of resistance. She curved her pliant body against his, devastatingly aware of an urgent male hunger that inflamed her own to white heat. Her tongue snaked sinuously into his mouth, fuelling the fires that would consume her.

But he was taking full control now, plundering the sweetest corners of her mouth with a fierce demand to which she could only submit. Her shawl had slid from her shoulders, and she felt his hands stroking down the length of her back to mould intimately over the base of her spine; his kisses scorched down into the sensitive hollows of her throat as her head tipped dizzily back.

She heard the roughened drag of his breathing, as harsh and ragged as her own; her spine was a quivering arc, every inch of her flesh craved his touch;

her mind was amazed by what was happening. His hand slid slowly up over her trembling body, and as his long, clever fingers curved over the swell of her breast she almost sobbed with pleasure.

With slow, warm sensuality he caressed her, arousing responses she didn't know how to control. As his mouth returned to claim hers again his hand slid inside her dress to smooth over her silken skin and find the tender bud of her nipple, teasing it until the exquisite sensation pierced her brain like incandescent wire.

He was leading her with consummate skill towards total surrender, his kisses warm and enticing, his caress stirring a wildness in her blood that she had never experience before. But then he lifted his head and looked down into her misted eyes.

'So, little Kate,' he murmured, his voice gravelly soft, 'are you ready to make do with second best after all?'

She stared up at him, uncomprehending—and then slowly memory flooded back, painfully. Hot tears of humiliation scalded her eyes, and she tore herself out of his arms. 'No,' she gasped. 'No way.'

His face hardened to a mask of stone. 'Run away, then,' he said contemptuously. 'Go on trying to hide, if you can. Just how long do you think you can go on fighting yourself? You can't keep that sexy little body on ice for ever, you know—not with the heat you generate.'

She struggled for control of her voice. 'I hate you,' she spat at him, vicious as a cat.

His cool laughter mocked her. 'Do you? It doesn't

seem to matter though, does it?'

Surging fury threatened to explode inside her skull. She longed for something heavy to throw at him, but all she could find was a cushion, so she threw that with all her strength, and then turned and bolted for the safety of her own cabin, slamming the door and leaning against it, the tears spilling over. He was right. Though she hated him, it didn't seem to matter. Even Dave had never aroused her to such a storm of desire.

She picked up the small photograph from the bedside shelf, and sat down on her bunk, staring at the smiling image, her heart torn by guilt as she realised that she was beginning to forget Dave in her growing obsession with Sean. She was being swept on irrevocably by the tide of time, and she was leaving him behind. Those short, happy months of their marriage were beginning to seem like the memory of a book she had once read.

She looked down regretfully at the photograph. 'I'm sorry, Dave,' she whispered. 'I can't help it.' She searched the smiling face for a hint of reproach. She had always done what Dave had wanted, never argued with him—except on the key issue of going to bed with him. She bit her lip, remembering all too vividly how helpless she had been in Sean's arms. She curled up on the bunk, clutching the photograph. She loved Dave. But when Sean McGregor touched her, even when he only looked at her . . .

She closed her eyes, living again the sensations of that tender caress, the flaming heat of that kiss. She was burning with the longing to surrender to the driving animal hunger he had awoken in her body.

4 FREE GAME TICKETS

One of which may already have won you up to

$1,000,000.⁰⁰

CASH!

THOUSANDS MORE CASH PRIZES

in the "Give Your Heart to Harlequin" Sweepstakes

Play it like a Lottery— And it's FREE!

IMMEDIATE REWARD

```
*  *  *  *  *  *  *  *  *  *  *  *  *  *  *  *  *  *  *  *  *  *  *  *
*    You may have already won a lifetime of cash         *
*    payments totaling up to $1,000,000.00!              *
*    Play our Sweepstakes Game -- Here's how...          *
*  *  *  *  *  *  *  *  *  *  *  *  *  *  *  *  *  *  *  *  *  *  *
```

On each of the first three tickets (numbered 1 to 3) there is a <u>silver area</u>. Using an eraser, rub off the silver box to reveal how much each ticket could be worth you must return the <u>entire</u> card to be eligible.

Each of the first three tickets also has a unique Sweepstakes number. When you return your game card, we'll check to see if your Sweepstakes numbers match any of the winning numbers already selected by our computer. If so, you'll win the amount shown under the rub-off area on that ticket. See official rules in back of this book for details.

Harlequin also invites you to participate in a new Sampling Project by accepting one or more totally FREE books! To request your free book(s), please rub off the area below the question mark on ticket 4 to reveal how many free books you will receive.

When you receive your free book(s), we hope you'll enjoy them and want to see more. So unless we hear from you, a month later we'll send you 8 additional novels. Each book is yours to keep for only $1.99 each -- 26¢ less per book than what you pay in stores. No charge for shipping and handling -- and of course, you may cancel any time.

Plus-you get a FREE MYSTERY GIFT!

If you return your game card with <u>all four silver areas</u> rubbed off, you will also receive a FREE Mystery Gift. It's your <u>immediate reward</u> for playing our Sweepstakes Game <u>and</u> sampling your free book(s).

P.S.

The first set of one or more books is FREE. So rub off the box on ticket 4 and return entire sheet of tickets!

If this is a winning ticket, it could be worth

1 **$1,000,000.00**
Rub off to reveal value if this is a winning ticket: ►

UNIQUE
SWEEPSTAKES
NUMBER: 906461AG

If this is a winning ticket, it could be worth

2 **$1,000,000.00**
Rub off to reveal value if this is a winning ticket: ►

UNIQUE
SWEEPSTAKES
NUMBER: 9062035L

If this is a winning ticket, it could be worth

3 **$1,000,000.00**
Rub off to reveal value if this is a winning ticket: ►

UNIQUE
SWEEPSTAKES
NUMBER: 906184WF

4 **ONE OR MORE FREE BOOKS**

HOW MANY FREE BOOKS?
Rub off to reveal number of free books you will receive ►

1672765559

"Give Your Heart To Harlequin" Sweepstakes

Yes! Enter my Sweepstakes Numbers in the Sweepstakes and let me
know if I've won a cash prize. If silver area on ticket 4 is rubbed off, I will
also receive one or more Harlequin Presents novels, free, along with a
Free Mystery Gift, as explained on the opposite page.   108 CIP CAMW

NAME

ADDRESS   APT.

CITY   STATE   ZIP CODE

Terms and prices subject to change.   NO PURCHASE NECESSARY

Printed in U.S.A.

**NO PURCHASE
NECESSARY**

Harlequin Presents®

901 Fuhrmann Blvd.
P.O. Box 1394
Buffalo, N.Y. 14240-1394

FIRST
CLASS
MAIL

There was a fundamental maleness in him that touched a deep core of feminine submissiveness inside her, far beyond the control of her rational mind.

She moaned softly, and turned her face into the coolness of the pillow. She had never dreamed that she could be capable of feeling such physical need, especially for a man she didn't love. It called into question everything she had ever believed about herself, about her values.

Once, it had all seemed so simple—love was a commitment of the heart, the mind, and the physical union that followed was an expression of that commitment. But with Sean, everything seemed to flow the other way. Their bodies communicated on a level that needed no involvement of the mind. And her heart was spinning in the vortex created by that powerful sexual force.

She wasn't in love with him. But her heart felt as if it were being torn in two, just the same. Why did it have to be Sean McGregor? Even if she could have been prepared to settle for what he was offering, her loyalty to Dave would hold her back.

And why had Sean let her off the hook so easily? If he only wanted to get her into his bed, he could have done that tonight, could have gone on kissing her until she was helpless to stop him. What was he trying to do? Make her admit that he wasn't second best?

Shaking her head to dismiss these troublesome thoughts, she got up from the bunk, and took off her dress. A warm, relaxing shower made her feel a little better, and slipping into her pyjamas she climbed into bed. But her dreams were troubled, and it was a very long night.

Kate could find no excuse for the cowardice that kept her in her own cabin until the middle of the following morning. That was all it was—cowardice, pure and simple. She woke as dawn tinged the sky with mother-of-pearl, but she lay in bed for hours, tossing restlessly, unwilling to go outside and face Sean, after the events of the previous evening.

A brisk rap on the door made her sit up quickly, her heart racing as she called anxiously, 'Yes?'

'Kate?' Are you all right? It's gone ten o'clock.' His voice was crisp and impersonal.

'Yes, I . . . I've got a bit of a headache, that's all,' she temporised quickly.

He laughed in mocking sympathy. 'Don't tell me you've got hangover!'

Kate smiled grimly. He had handed her a ready-made excuse for her weakness last night. 'Well, I did have rather a lot of wine,' she claimed with minimal regard for the truth. 'I'm not used to drinking.'

'I see.' There was a terse note in his voice. 'Would you like some coffee?'

'Yes, please.'

'Black?'

'Yes, please,' she agreed with a grimace. She hated black coffee. She heard his receding footsteps beyond the closed door. When he returned, she had buried herself beneath the coverlet, hoping that he wouldn't notice that her colour was as healthy as ever.

'Just put it on the floor,' she begged, making her

voice weak with self-pity.

'I didn't realise you'd had that much to drink last night.' He sounded as if he wasn't entirely convinced by her act.

She peeped up at him cautiously between her lashes. He was standing over her, his arms folded across his broad chest, his expression grim.

'I told you, I'm not used to it,' she defended nervously.

'I see. No doubt that accounts for your uncharacteristic behaviour.'

'I'm afraid I don't really remember much about it,' she mumbled, her cheeks flushing.

'Well, if you're that ill, you'd better stay in bed,' he advised her coldly. 'If you've no objection, I'll leave you to find your own way around. I have other things to do today.'

'Fine,' agreed Kate, irrationally annoyed. Surely that was just what she wanted?

'I'll leave you the door-code. Mind you don't forget it,' he went on in a crisp tone. 'I'm not sure when I'll be back. Maybe not until tomorrow. Will you be all right on your own?'

'Of course.'

'Right. I'll see you when I see you then. Goodbye.'

'Goodbye,' she responded with studied indifference. She lay back on the bunk, staring up at the ceiling. Where was he going? To spend the day with the lovely Georgina? ... And the night? Well, so what? She didn't care. At least it meant he would leave her alone.

The sound of Sean's footsteps across the aft-deck

above her told Kate that he had left the boat. She got up, dressed casually in a pair of jeans and a T-shirt, and then walked through to the galley and tipped her unwanted black coffee down the sink. She made herself some breakfast, and ate it with guilty haste, afraid that Sean would come back and catch her out in her lies.

It seemed strange to be on the boat by herself. She washed up her breakfast things, and went back into the saloon. Now that she knew it was a private yacht, not for charter-hire, the touches of luxury took on even more significance. Sean plainly enjoyed a hedonistic lifestyle when sailing. There was a well stocked library of music and books, reflecting the best of modern taste. The navigation and communication system had all the latest technological wizardry.

Drawn by curiosity, she wandered back down to the forward cabins, and stood staring at Sean's door, remembering the glimpse she had seen on that first tour of inspection. Almost of its own volition her hand lifted—the door opened. The cabin was as uncompromisingly masculine as its owner. The big bed was covered in a Mondrian patchwork of spice-coloured suede, the thick carpet was a rich sienna brown, the walls gleaming dark Africn mahogany.

On one wall was a display of framed colour photographs, and Kate moved closer to study them. They were all of Sean with various groups of friends, posing with prize catches of big fish. Some of them dated back as far as his teenage years, the faces bright and young and optimistic. He had changed little— there was the same quirky smile—and yet ...

somehow he had changed totally, in a way that mere passing years couldn't explain.

As she examined the photographs, she realised that she was looking at a broken sequence. Two whole years were not represented. And it was in those two years that the subtle changes had occurred. A hardness had crept into the line of the mouth, cynicism had replaced youthful pride in those level blue eyes.

Unexpectedly a tear welled up into the corner of her eye. Something had scarred Sean in those two years—and it was something to do with Dave. But what? She was no nearer to guessing the answer to the riddle. Deep in thought, she wandered back up to the sunny deck.

'Ahoy there, *Barracuda*!'

Kate glanced up to see Serge François waving to her from the quayside, confident of his welcome. He was wearing a pale blue jogging-suit, the top unzipped to display a thick thatch of dark hair across his chest, highlighted by a flash of gold chain round his neck.

'Hello,' she said, hoping the lack of enthusiasm in her voice did not sound ill-mannered. Not that he was likely to notice, she reflected wryly.

'Sean is not here?' he asked.

'Not at the moment,' she admitted unwillingly.

'Ah!' He invited himself abroad the boat. Kate sat down, hoping he was not going to come too close. 'What do you do with yourself today, *chérie*?' he enquired, his dark eyes ablaze with Gallic charm.

'Oh, I'm going to be quite busy,' she answered quickly. 'I have to write up my notes while everything is still fresh in my mind.'

'Oh,' he pouted. 'Could you not leave that today, and come water-skiing with me?'

'I'm afraid not.'

'But then you must have dinner with me,' he insisted. 'You cannot work all the time—you must eat, after all.'

Kate hesitated, her mind racing as she sought for an excuse, but none presented itself. 'Thank you,' she said with a demure smile. 'I'd be delighted.'

'It will be entirely my pleasure,' he throbbed huskily. 'Shall we say eight o'clock? I shall anticipate with impatience.'

He took her hand, and kissed the tips of her fingers, and then stepped lightly back onto the quayside. Kate watched him jog lithely back towards the hotel, pausing as he went to exchange greetings with some of the guests, sign a few autographs. He was plainly conscious of the admiring glances of the women. He was certainly good-looking, she thought in a detached way, but not her type at all. He was too dark, too contrived. Her taste ran to sun-bleached hair and cool blue eyes.

Where was Sean now? Making love to Georgina on some secluded beach? More fool her if she let him, Kate thought with savage satisfaction. Didn't she realise she was no more than another notch on his belt? It wouldn't be anything special to him.

But all day, she sat in the sunshine trying to write up her notes, her mind strayed again to images of Sean and Georgina together, until she was forced to admit that she was jealous.

She dressed for dinner in her ice-pink dress, a necklace of tiny luminescent shells at her throat. At least Sean was certain to learn of her dining with Serge, and realise that she had not spent the day pining for him.

She waited for Serge on deck, not wanting to give him any excuse to come aboard, and as she saw him walking along the quayside she stepped across the gangway and went to meet him.

He took her hands, and gazed down warmly into her eyes. 'Ah, *ma chérie*,' he murmured throatily. '*Ravissante.*'

Kate suppressed a smile of wry humour. She suspected that he kept calling her '*chérie*' because he couldn't remember her name. He was certainly the epitome of male elegance in black dinner jacket and frilled evening shirt, and he moved with conscious grace. His self-absorption was almost magnificent.

As they walked into the dining-room, Kate's eyes swept swiftly round the tables, though she refused to admit to herself that she was looking for Sean. He wasn't there, and neither was Georgina, and as Serge led her to their table her smile was a little over-bright.

'So,' he began when the waiter had taken their order. 'Tell me, what is this sunken treasure you are seeking?'

His tone was mildly patronising, and Kate had to quell a surge of irritation. She told him briefly about her project, aware that she had only half his attention. His eyes were roving around the room, smiling at every passable female in sight.

The waiter brought their starter, and Serge turned

on her the full kilowatt power of his charm. 'But, yes. It sounds quite fascinating,' he declared, though Kate was sure he had hardly been listening to her.

'How long are you appearing here?' she asked, guessing that she was turning the conversation to his favourite topic.

'This time I am here for just three weeks,' he told her. 'Then, alas, I must return to Los Angeles. I have an album to record, and possibly a television series.' He went on, talking about himself, telling her about his career. His monologue was peppered with many amusing anecdotes and Kate felt as if she were watching an oft-repeated and very smoothly delivered performance. But she laughed in all the right places, glad to be able to relax and let the evening drift past her.

Suddenly out of the corner of her eye she spotted a fluttery movement, and a gleam of blonde hair. It was Georgina. She was with a party of guests who were erupting noisily into the room, their bright sun-clothes and the souvenir coral they were clutching suggesting that they had just returned from a day trip. Many of them had plainly sampled a quantity of the potent Bahamian punches, and Georgina was having some difficulty in settling them at their tables while maintaining that sweet, feminine image.

Without consulting Kate, Serge beckoned to her as she crossed the room, and she accepted the chair he held for her with a grateful smile. 'Phew! I'm bushed!' she declared inelegantly as she sat down.

'Had a busy day?' enquired Serge sympathetically. 'Have some wine.'

'Thanks. I swear, one of these days I'm going to end up shoving one of those creeps over the side.'

Serge laughed. 'You have been to the Sea Gardens?'

'How did you guess?' she returned with a sigh. 'Thirteen hours of it. Half-eight this morning we set off, and now it's—what, nearly ten o'clock? Serge, I tell you, it's too much. Always it's the same dialogue. "Gee, look, the boat's got a glass bottom. Why don't you walk across it, honey? Give the fish a thrill." I swear, one day I'll just go crazy!'

She rambled on, but Kate wasn't listening. Her mind was filled with just one thought. Wherever else he had been all day, Sean hadn't been making love with Georgina.

Serge's voice cut across her thoughts. 'I regret very much that I must leave two such lovely ladies,' he purred. 'But it is time that I must work a little for my living. I will return with promptitude.' He favoured each with a warm, intimate smile, and then with an elegant little bow walked away.

'Dishy, isn't he?' remarked Georgina in a friendly tone.

'Oh . . . yes,' agreed Kate automatically.

'And he knows it,' added Georgina with a dry laugh.

Kate glanced at her in surprise, and then she laughed too, nodding. 'He does rather, doesn't he?' she agreed.

Georgina smiled at her. 'You're here with Sean, aren't you?' she asked.

'That's right,' confirmed Kate, glad that the

subdued lighting would hide the soft blush that rose to her cheeks.

Georgina smiled wryly. 'Ah, now that's what I call a real man,' she sighed. 'Serge is dead jealous of him, of course. He's always trying to pinch his women. Oh . . . no offence,' she added quickly.

Kate returned the smile. 'Oh, that's all right,' she said. 'I was under no illusions. But as it happens in this case Serge is wrong. I'm not one of Sean's women.'

Georgina cast her a doubting look. 'You were dancing with him last night for long enough,' she remarked drily.

'Yes, well I . . . we . . .'

Georgina laughed. 'Oh, don't bother trying to explain,' she said sympathetically. 'I think every woman he meets falls in love with him. I'm absolutely crazy about him myself. But be warned. He's strictly the love 'em and leave 'em sort. Don't let him break your heart.' Her smile was brittle with self-mockery, and Kate felt a little sorry for her.

'Have you known him a long time?' she asked.

'About two years,' said Georgina, 'but I couldn't say I really know him very well. I don't think anybody does. He's a very private person.' Kate leaned forward, interested, and Georgina went on, 'I know he grew up in Nassau. His father died when he was quite young, and he and his mother lived with his grandfather. I believe his mother eventually remarried—she lives in Miami now, but he sees her quite a lot. It's his grandfather that's important—I think he's the only person he really cares about in the world. He comes over to see him every few weeks.'

'His grandfather lives here?'

'Round the other side of the island. He retired here about ten years ago, and left Sean to run the business. We don't see much of him—he's very old, in a wheelchair. The McGregors have lived on this island for generations, and when the old man made all his money he bought it. There was another hotel here then, but it was flattened by a particularly bad hurricane a few years ago, so Sean had this one built in its place.'

'I didn't think Sean had much to do with running the hotels,' remarked Kate.

'Oh, he likes to give that impression,' said Georgina. 'He says he hires the best staff, and leaves them to get on with their job. But he always knows exactly what's going on, and if there's trouble anywhere he just shows up, as if by magic, and sorts it out. He can be pretty ruthless if anyone tries to mess him about, but the staff that have been here for a long time think he's the greatest. And I'll tell you, I've worked in a lot of hotels, but this one's the friendliest and the smoothest run of any I've ever known.'

Kate sat back, trying to absorb this new information into the constantly changing picture of Sean she was building in her mind.

The band had left the stage, and Serge walked into the spotlight as his pianist rippled lightly over the chords. He was resplendent in his stage clothes, and Georgina laughed softly. 'Who's a pretty boy then?'

Kate laughed with her, amazed that she could so quickly feel such friendliness towards a woman to whom she had felt nothing but venom for the past twenty-four hours. Serge rejoined them when he had finished his cabaret act, and Kate danced with him for a while, and then let him walk her back through the gardens to the yacht marina.

At the *Barracuda's* berth she paused, and smiled up at Serge rather warily. 'Well, good night,' she said. 'Thank you for a lovely evening.' He looked down at her questioningly. 'I'd invite you aboard for a coffee,' she added, mentally crossing her fingers, 'but Sean might be asleep.'

A flicker of uncertainty passed behind his eyes. 'Ah, of course,' he murmured. 'But I will see you tomorrow, yes? Perhaps you will like to come water-skiing with me?'

'Well, I'm not sure . . .'

'I shall come for you at eleven o'clock,' he said, as if he had not even heard her demur. 'Good night, *ma chérie.*'

He tilted up her chin with one finger, and his head bent over her. Reluctantly she let him kiss her; it wasn't exactly unpleasant, but she found herself remembering the way Sean had kissed her. There was just no comparison.

After few moments she decided he was getting little too carried away, so as politely as she could she disentangled herself from his arms, 'I really should go in now,' she said demurely. 'Good night.'

He gave her melting look, but made no further attempt to detain her. Lifting her hand to his lips, he kissed her fingers. 'Good night, then,' he murmured. 'Sleep well, *ma chérie.* I will see you tomorrow.'

He walked away with a jaunty step. She watched

him go, her lips curving with amusement. He really was impervious! But she would have to try to think of an excuse not to go water-skiing with him. He was perfectly capable of running them aground on some isolated beach, and she could guess that he would be easily able to convince himself that any resistance on her part was mere coyness.

Quietly she stepped down on to the deck of the *Barracuda*, her heart beginning to beat unsteadily as she wondered if Sean had returned. Would he have seen her kissing Serge? And if he had? It was too much to hope that he might be jealous. But when she let herself into the saloon cabin, the silence told her that she was alone. Holding her breath, she crept forward to the steps leading down towards the galley. There was no sound. On tiptoe she approached the door to his cabin and slid it open. It was empty.

She scuttled back to her own cabin quickly in case he should return and catch her prowling, and in a few moments she was curled up in bed in her pyjamas.

CHAPTER SEVEN

SHE woke early, to find that Sean had not returned. As it was Sunday she dressed a little more smartly than usual, in a white cotton skirt, and a pretty embroidered top, and took her breakfast up on deck. It was another perfect morning. The sun was climbing a sky of pure, vivid blue, and the sea was as smooth as silk.

Kate breathed in the fresh, salty air with a contented sigh. Serge was only a minor problem. Tomorrow they would be sailing again. Just for a little while, all on her own, she could indulge herself with idle daydreams, seeing in her mind's eye that lean, muscular body, perfectly braced against the motion of the boat as he moved around the deck.

When she heard his voice she thought it was part of her dream, until he said again, 'Kate?' She turned quickly. He was standing on the quayside, wearing only a pair of frayed and faded denim shorts, his hands on his hips. Her heart skidded and began to beat far too fast. 'Fancy going for a sail?' he asked casually. 'I'd like you to meet an old friend of mine.'

'Oh, I . . . I was going water-skiing wih Serge,' she dissembled, her colour rising.

He lifted one eyebrow in faint amusement. 'Fallen for the Gallic charm, have you?' he taunted.

'No,' she protested quickly. 'I just . . . .'

'Then leave him a note,' he suggested promptly.

110

Under the spell of those hypnotic blue eyes she couldn't think of a single thing to say. 'All right,' she mumbled. 'I won't be long.' Ten minutes later she was walking with Sean along the quayside, a bright beach-bag over her shoulder, leaving a brief apology to Serge stuck to the door of the *Barracuda's* cabin.

'This way,' said Sean. 'Careful. Don't fall in.'

Kate glanced down at the small inflatable dinghy bobbing on the water, and back up at Sean in cool amusement. 'Fall in?' she repeated. 'Me? I've been messing about in boats since I was so high.'

'There's a first time for everything,' he teased, mischief dancing in his eyes.

'We'll, this isn't it,' she declared confidently, 'as long as you don't push me.'

'I wouldn't dream of it,' he promised, adopting an innocent expression and standing back as she climbed carefully into the little boat and moved forward to settle herself in the bows, her beach-bag between her feet. The boat was so small that as Sean sat in the stern he had to stretch his long legs on each side of hers, his hair-roughened calf brushing against her smooth skin. She tried very hard to take no notice.

He started the powerful outboard motor, and they swept swiftly out of the harbour, neatly avoiding all the other marine traffic. Once out in open water, Sean steered away from the hotel, passing in a wide curve round the western tip of the island to traverse its southern shore, where the graceful palm trees grew right down to the sea and a maze of sand-banks and coral stands patterned the dancing green water with lacy wavelets.

Sean steered the small boat skilfully through the twisting channels, and Kate watched in fascination as a school of silvery fan-tail mullets, moving as one, darted out from the shadow of the hull, or the diaphanous blue parachute of a poisonous jellyfish drifted by.

But though she avoided looking up at the man sitting so close to her, her awareness of him was overwhelming. She sought in vain for something to say, some kind of small talk to make her appear as if she were at ease, but her mind would not focus. She felt far too vulnerable—she should never have agreed to come with him.

A sudden flash of silver alongside the boat startled her, and Sean laughed. 'He's come to meet us,' he said, his voice rich with pleasure.

Kate looked round quickly, and gasped as a sleek shape darted alongside again and vanished. The next moment a benignly smiling face lifted out of the water, and a dark eye regarded her with friendly curiosity. 'A dolphin!' she cried in delight.

'This is Salty,' Sean told her, leaning out to stroke the smooth head affectionately. She stared in wonder, instantly captivated by the dolphin's spell. They had sailed into a sheltered lagoon, where a tiny beach of pink coral sand sloped gently into the tranquil blue water.

Salty began to nudge playfully at the boat, rocking it violently. 'OK, Salty, I'm coming,' said Sean. 'Don't overturn the dinghy.' He cut the outboard motor, and let the boat run in towards the shore under its own momentum. A few yards from the shore he stood up, and let himself fall lazily over the side, making a terrific splash, and as Kate watched, he sank to the bottom.

The dolphin turned swiftly, and swam down to him, and lifted him gently back to the surface. Kate applauded the 'rescue' enthusiastically, and Salty lifted his head out of the water and nodded as if in acknowledgement.

The boat ran aground with a gentle crunch over the sharp sand, and Kate jumped out to pull it safely up the beach. The dolphin was frolicking in the crystal clear water; out of sheer exuberance he would leap into the air in a shower of sparkling droplets, soaring in an effortless arc to slice back into the water with barely a ripple. Sometimes he would flip over and crash down on his back, stunning the water with all his two hundred pounds in weight.

He even let Sean ride his back, gripping his dorsal fin, twisting and plunging to dislodge him, and then coming back to do it again. Kate watched a little enviously. 'Would he let me do that?' she asked.

'I don't know,' said Sean. 'You're a stranger. Try it and see.'

Quickly she stripped down to her bikini, and ran into the water. At once Salty moved away, cautious. 'Stand still,' said Sean, moving towards her and watching as the dolphin circled warily a few yards way. She waited, all her attention on the sleek animal, and when Sean caught her and tipped her neatly back into the water she went under in spluttering protest, her arms flailing wildly in a useless attempt to regain her balance.

She came up laughing, and kicked a shower of spray into Sean's face. He caught her feet, but she was wet and slippery and easily able to twist out of his grasp. He began to chase her, and Salty came to join the fun, rising beneath Kate to knock her off-balance again and then, as Sean cheered, he turned with a flick of his graceful tail to knock him over too.

'Thank you, Salty,' Kate laughed, gasping for her breath. They played like childen, and at last, flattered by her unstinting admiration, Salty allowed Kate to grip his fin, and took her on a twisting, splashing ride around the lagoon.

He deposited her back beside Sean, and let her stroke his smoothly domed head. 'Oh, but you're beautiful!' she breathed, in reverence for this creature so intelligent and yet so playful, so peaceful.

'I thought you'd like him,' remarked Sean, his eyes following the dolphin's effortless display of aquabatic skills until, with a last spectacular leap, he was gone, vanishing beyond the coral barrier towards the open sea.

Kate sighed sadly and began to wade up out of the water to where the boat was beached. 'I've never been that close to a dolphin before,' she said, pulling a big, fluffy beach towel from her bag and beginning to rub her hair dry. 'How long have you known him?'

'About five years. He just swims into the lagoon whenever he feels like it. Sometimes he'll hang around for a month or more, another time he'll stay only a few hours.'

'Has he always been this tame?'

'I don't think "tame" is really the word for it,'

mused Sean. 'He chooses his friends, but if he decides to trust you he'll share a joy for living that mankind seems to have forgotten all about.'

Kate lifted her eyes to his face, studying its strong lines as if seeing it for the first time. She had been wrong about so much—it seemed she had misjudged him completely. She had thought him a hardened cynic, wanting only to use her for his fleeting pleasure. Could she have been wrong about that too?

He seemed to read the question in her eyes. 'Kate?' he murmured, laying one hand along her cheek. She bent her head and brushed her lips tremblingly over the vibrant pulse inside his wrist. 'Kate!' His fingers twisted in her hair, and for a long moment their eyes met and held. Then slowly he bent his head over hers, and their warm breath mingled, their lips melted together.

He found no resistance as his tongue swept into the secret, sensitive corners of her mouth, stirring that wild, wanton response in her blood. She reached up, wrapping her arms tightly round his neck, and his hands moulded her pliant body to the hard length of his. The scattering of sun-bleached hair on his chest and thighs chafed against her soft skin.

His kiss was deep, demanding, and she offered everything she had. Her pulse thundered in her ears, drowning out any last whisper of warning her rational mind may have uttered. His arms had folded around her, sweeping her up, and her head swam dizzily as he laid her back gently on the sharp sand.

Her bikini top seemed to melt away, and she felt his hands stroking down the length of her bare back, felt the warm roughness of male skin against the silkiness of her naked breasts. A tremor of exquisite pleasure shimmered through her, communicating vividly to him her total arousal.

With a low growl he rolled on top of her, crushing her deliciously beneath his weight. Their mouths broke reluctantly apart to draw breath, and his hot kisses began to explore the delicate shell of her ear, the sensitive hollow of her throat. His hard jaw rasped over her skin, his caressing hands inflamed her response wherever they touched, and she moved beneath him in sensuous invitation.

In slow torment his lips moved down over the aching ripeness of her breasts, tracing a flame path of kisses. His tongue swirled in languorous circles around the rose-pink peaks, and then his mouth closed over one tender nipple and began to suckle gently until she moaned with the sheer pleasure of it. Her hands curled in his hair, and her body curved against his in urgent hunger.

He lifted his head and looked down into her face, his eyes blazing with a fire that scorched her brain. His hands slid down over the smooth plane of her stomach, the slender curve of her thigh, and then trailed back up over the silken skin to seek the most intimate of caresses.

She quivered in response, ready to surrender—but as he began to gently ease down the briefs of her bikini she froze in sudden panic, a thousand doubts and questions swirling into her mind.

'No!' she gasped on a faint breath, trying to pull away from him.

'What?' His eyes changed as he registered her last-minute refusal, and suddenly she was fighting him, struggling to escape him as he pinned her down in the sand. 'What the hell kind of game are you playing now?' he snarled savagely.

'Let me go,' she pleaded in a desperate whisper.

'Oh, just like that?' he sneered coldly. 'Switch on, switch off, just when you say so? Oh, no, little Kate. That isn't how it's going to be.'

She lunged away from him, but he caught her in an imprisoning hold, trapping her right arm beneath his body and catching the other in an iron grip at the wrist. Then with his free hand he began to strip off her bikini briefs. She twisted and kicked, but he was far too strong for her, and he didn't seem to care if he hurt her.

Her struggles were useless, and she sobbed in bitter defeat, 'I hate you.'

'You said that already,' he reminded her tauntingly.

'Do you think raping me is going to make me feel any different?'

His laughter mocked her. 'Oh, I'm not going to rape you, little Kate. I've never forced a woman in my life, and I'll be damned if I'm going to start with you. No, I'm just going to teach you a little lesson, and I don't think you'll forget it in a hurry.'

Her body lay helpless beneath his hand as he held her down, and began to inflict a slow torture of sensuality, intimate caresses of such exquisite skill that she felt herself dissolving in languid rapture, try as she might to control herself. Her breath was hot on her lips, and she closed her eyes on swirling darkness, and still he led her on.

He was playing with her responses until she had no more secrets left, no more will to fight him, defeated by a pleasure so intense that it flooded her whole being with a melting heat. But at the moment of final surrender she heard only his cruel laughter, and abruptly he pushed her away. Bereft, devastated, she curled up into a ball of despair, and sobbed her heart out into the sand.

It took a long time for Kate to recover some semblance of composure. As her tears subsided she became aware of Sean standing close to her. He dropped her bikini into the sand beside her. 'Get dressed,' he ordered coldly. 'We're eating lunch up at the house, with my grandfather.'

Kate stared up at him bleakly. She couldn't face meeting anyone, not yet. 'I'd really rather . . .'

'I really don't care what you'd rather do,' he interrupted her cuttingly. 'He's expecting us. You'll have the good manners to accept his invitation.'

She flushed with embarrassment. For a moment she wondered if she dare defy him, take the dinghy and return to the *Barracuda* alone. But he forestalled her in a voice that would brook no disobedience, 'Don't even think about it,' he warned harshly.

Her eyes flashed cold fury. 'Very well, I'll come,' she said, her voice sharp with resentment.

'And you can take that tone out of your voice,' he added threateningly. 'I'll not have him troubled, is that clear? You'll behave as if there's never been any more between us than a simple business relationship.'

'That suits me fine,' she retaliated bitterly. 'That's all I wanted from the start.'

'Oh, yes?' he sneered, his voice a whiplash of contempt. 'You asked for everything you got. And you can think yourself lucky I let you off so lightly.'

She flinched under his scorn, and turned away from him, her throat tight with tears. Quickly she pulled on her clothes over her bikini, and tugged a comb through her almost-dry curls. Then she picked up her towel and shook the sand out of it, and folding it carefully put it back into her beach-bag.

By the time she had done all that she felt a little more composed, and turned back to Sean, who was waiting for her impatiently. 'Ready?' he grated.

She nodded, and he turned on his heel and walked away through the trees, leaving her to hurry after him. She dreaded the prospect ahead of her, but she would hide her feelings—and not only because he had so high-handedly commanded it. Her innate good breeding would not let her be rude to an old man who, she must confess, she had an enormous curiosity to meet.

The path led up a rough stairway hewn by nature out of the grey green rock, to a small white clapboard bungalow that looked out over the open sea. A wide verandah ran along the front of it, and beneath its shelter sat a very old man in a high-backed cane wheelchair, a tartan blanket tucked round his legs.

Kate thought at first that he was asleep, but as they drew closer she realised that she was being subjected to a searching scrutiny from a pair of eyes as blue and all-seeing as Sean's. She returned his gaze levelly as she stepped up on to the porch.

'Well, well. Good afternoon,' he said. His voice had lost none of its vigour, though his hair was pure white, and the skin that covered the craggy bones of his face was like crumpled parchment. 'So, you're Kate Taylor, are you. Well, you're welcome here.'

He extended his left hand, and Kate shook it awkwardly. 'You'll have to excuse me for not shaking hands properly,' he told her mischievously. He lifted his right arm from the folds of the blanket, and Kate realised with a shock that it ended in a stump.

'Mislaid my damn hand forty-odd years ago,' he explained gleefully. 'Forgot the first rule of a shark-hunter—always make sure your shark is good and dead before you swing it in-board.' He laughed at Kate's horrorstruck expression. 'Oh, it was just a little tiddler,' he went on proudly. 'Tiger-shark, no more than ten or twelve feet long. Gave us some good sport, though—played him all morning before we landed him. And then, just as I'm about to slit him open—snap! He takes my hand off, knife and all!'

'What did you do?' asked Kate with a shudder.

'What did I do?' He chuckled richly. 'I cussed him, that's what I did!'

Kate joined in his laughter. 'I'm not surprised,' she said. 'But how did you kill him?'

'Oh, that was his last move,' he told her. 'After that he really was finished.' Abruptly he turned to his grandson. 'You didn't tell me she was such a pretty little thing,' he scolded him.

'Didn't I?' returned Sean blandly.

'You're a young dog,' the old man grumbled with satisfaction. 'Go and make yourself respectable. You know what Martha will say if she sees you walking round in those tatty old shorts in front of this young lady. Can't you see she's not one of your usual fluffy little pieces?'

'Quite,' agreed Sean drily. He glanced down at Kate, his blue eyes conveying nothing. 'If you'll excuse me, I'll go and get changed. Lunch will be ready in just a little while.'

Kate flickered him a minimal response, aware that the old man was watching them and sensing the undercurrent of tension. When Sean had gone, he turned back to her and said, 'Well, sit down then, girl, if you're stopping.'

'Thank you, Mr McGregor,' smiled Kate.

'Oh, good heavens, call me Nat,' he insisted impatiently. 'When a pretty young woman calls me Mr McGregor it makes me feel old.' 'I can hardly believe that,' responded Kate with a smile. In spite of his years, the old man was still an incorrigible flirt. He must have been a very big hit with the ladies when he was younger, she reflected. Like his grandson.

He was regarding her with sharp curiosity. 'So,' he began. 'You're looking for the wreck of that damn pirate ship again?'

'Yes,' answered Kate.

'And how did you manage to persuade my grandson to help you?'

Kate met his probing gaze frankly. 'I'm afraid I misunderstood things a little,' she explained. 'I knew nothing about him except his name, which I'd found in my late husband's log-books. I had assumed he hired out his boat on a charter basis.'

'Oh, you did? Your husband didn't tell you anything about him then?'

'Nothing at all,' she said firmly. 'Even when we first arrived at the hotel I had no idea his family owned it.'

He nodded thoughtfully. Then slowly he smiled, apparently satisfied. Kate wondered if he had suspected that she was a gold-digger, or if he knew something of the quarrel between Sean and Dave.

After a moment she became aware that she was being watched, and looked up. Sean was leaning against the frame of the door, now dressed in jeans and a checked shirt. She turned her eyes away swiftly, her heartbeat racing.

'Martha says I'm to show you where you can wash your hands, before lunch,' he said, grinning with a trace of self-mockery as if the unseen Martha had sent him on his errand like a small boy.

'Thank you.' She stood up, and slung her beach-bag over her shoulder. 'Excuse me,' she said to Nat. 'I won't be long.'

'You'd better not be,' he warned portentously. 'Martha gets hopping mad if a meal's kept waiting, and I'd rather face a hurricane than Martha in a taking, any day of the week!'

Kate laughed. She was quite sure that the indomitable old man had never been afraid of anyone in his life. Sean led her through a neat hallway, with floorboards that gleamed from years of polish, to a corridor at the back of the house.

'Here you are,' he said, opening the door to an old-fashioned bathroom. 'You've no need to rush. Martha said lunch won't be ready for another twenty minutes.'

'Good. I'd like to wash the salt water out of my hair—it gets horribly sticky if you leave it,' she said, trying to match his impersonal tone.

'Make yourself at home,' he invited with cool hospitality.

She stepped past him awkwardly, not looking up at him. He was speaking to her with the formal politeness of a stranger, and she could almost feel the coldness emanating from him. She was relieved when he went away. She closed the door, pulled off her embroidered top, and filled the sink with warm water to rinse her hair.

Fifteen minutes later, her hair scrubbed vigorously dry and curling riotously round her head, she was ready to go back outside. She could hear the two men talking as she walked through the shadowy hall. Sean was leaning against the low rail that ran along the front of the porch, and as she looked at him Kate realised that she was seeing the face she had seen in those earliest old photographs, all trace of that hard cynicism gone. He was smiling down at his grandfather, and there was a warmth in his blue eyes that made her heart contract.

But as he glanced up and saw her standing just inside the hall his features set into those familiar uncompromising lines. Kate felt an odd little stab of disappointment.

Nat McGregor smiled up at her mischievously. 'Ah, that's what I like to see,' he approved with a chuckle. 'A woman who doesn't need to spend hours tatting herself up.'

'Now then, Mr Nat,' came a scolding voice behind

Kate. 'Time to stop all this chattering. You come on inside now and have your lunch.'

Kate turned as a portly island woman in a yellow flowered dress waddled out on to the porch, and laid her big, purposeful hands on the wheelchair. Her voice was pure, musical Bahamian, the consonants softened and flowing like honey.

'Stop nagging me, woman,' protested Nat grumpily. 'Aren't you going to say good afternoon to our guest?'

The housekeeper turned her eyes to Kate. 'Good afternoon to you,' she said coldly.

Kate was stunned by the unexpected wave of hostility she sensed from the woman, as chilling as the response she had received from old Joshua on the boat. 'Good afternoon,' she managed to say, extending her hand politely. Martha ignored it, and began fussing to negotiate the wheelchair through the doorway. Kate let her hand drop to her side, embarrassed.

'Martha rules the roost around here,' Nat informed her in a stage whisper.

'Oh, go on with you, Mr Nat,' chuckled Martha affectionately.

'You look very well on it,' smiled Kate warmly, bending swiftly to tuck in a trailing corner of the blanket. Martha was watching her, her black eyes narrowed and suspicious. Kate tried to smile at her, but her cheeks felt stiff and she knew that she was blushing. She stood back, and followed the housekeeper's stately progress into the house.

Martha's attitude puzzled her, as had Joshua's. Of course, it was to be expected that Sean's people would take his side in his quarrel with Dave—but that their rancour should still linger, a year after Dave's death, and so strongly that it soured the natural friendliness of the Bahamian people, was odd. What could have aroused such bitter feelings?

The lunch was delicious—fresh crabs, baked in their shells, seasoned with sweet peppers. Sean and his grandfather chatted lazily to each other. And it was only the occasional sardonic gleam in Sean's change-able blue eyes when they rested on her that reminded her that the things that had happened on the beach had not been a figment of her fevered imagination.

Old Nat McGregor was a fascinating man. He had lived through wild times, and had known personally all the legendary old gangsters who were only characters in films to Kate. Eagerly she prompted him to tell tales of those exciting years when he had run the gauntlet of the American coastguard to make his illicit fortune.

'Not now,' he apologised regretfuly. 'I'm an old man, and I have to take a little nap after my lunch. But later—there'll be plenty of time.'

Kate glanced questioningly at Sean. 'We're not sailing until tomorrow morning,' he reminded her coolly. 'We can spend the night here.'

Her eyes flashed in anger at his high-handed manners, but the warning glance he slanted towards her quelled her words of protest. So she had to seeth in silence until Martha came to take Nat away for his rest. As soon as they were alone, she burst out furiously, 'You didn't tell me I was staying the night.'

He shrugged and rose to his feet. She followed him

out on to the front porch, needled by his coolness. 'I want to go back to the *Barracuda* tonight,' she insisted contrarily.

'Why?' he asked, blandly ignoring her irritation. 'Martha can find you anything you need for the night.'

'I didn't want to come here,' she protested unsteadily. 'I don't want to stay.'

'I thought you wanted to hear my grandfather's stories?' he mocked, his eyes as cold as flints. 'He enjoys telling them, and he doesn't get many visitors.'

'I do, but . . .' She turned away from him, unable to frame her words.

'We're staying,' he said with an air of finality. 'Don't worry, I shall keep well out of your way. There won't be any repetition of that torrid little scene on the beach. From now on, you can rest assured that I have no wish to touch you.'

She heard him walk swiftly away, and turned in time to see him vanish the way they had come, back towards the beach. Her legs weakened beneath her, and she sat down on the top step of the porch, leaning against the rail, tears trickling down her cheeks.

What was the matter with her? She was reacting as if she were in love with him. But she couldn't be—it was impossible. Not a man like that, who had treated her with such humiliating contempt. And yet she knew that her wanton behaviour had warranted such punishment. She should never have let things go that far. He had done no more than turn the tables on her.

And in spite of what he had said, she knew that if she were to let him see she were prepared to accept what he was offering, he would respond. But all he was offering was a casual fling, a brief affair for the duration of the voyage. Could she settle for just that?

And what of his quarrel with Dave? She still didn't know the cause of it. The question flared in the forefront of her mind, extinguishing all other thoughts. She had to know.

She glanced around. The house was quiet, except for Martha singing somwhere in the distant kitchen regions. Sean was nowhere in sight, and his grandfather was asleep. If there were any clues to be found here, in Sean's home, now would be her only chance to find them.

CHAPTER EIGHT

SHE hesitated, unwilling to snoop when she was a guest in the house. But her tangled emotions overcame her reluctance. Her breathing was ragged as she rose to her feet, and tiptoed silently through the quiet hall into the sitting-room.

It was a big room, on the corner of the house, with windows looking out over the open sea. The floor gleamed with a rich patina of years of wax polish on good English oak; the deep chairs were upholstered in dark green leather that had become a little scuffed with age—not out of neglect, the atmosphere of the room proclaimed, but out of a reluctance to change anything that was much loved. There was an air of deep contentment here, of tranquillity. It was a place to be happy.

There were trinkets on the polished tables, fading photographs in silver frames, trophies collected by an old man in a lifetime of adventure.

One long wall was lined with bookshelves, and Kate trailed along it, examining the contents. Among the books were stacks of magazines, shoe boxes crammed with old letters. And a pile of photograph albums—some old, some not so old.

She opened one idly—it was full of fading sepia prints of young girls in flapper dresses and sharp-looking men in double-breasted suits. She opened another: a young Sean on the water front at Nassau, a huge blue shark at his feet; Sean in football kit, proudly holding a big silver cup.

She turned the pages. These were his college years—laughing young faces, with that easy confidence that rich kids seem to acquire early. Groups of friends aboard a boat—smaller than the *Barracuda* but carrying the same name.

And there, very much at home among the smiling faces, was Dave—page after page, as other faces came and went, Dave was there. The last picture was of the two young men, grinning into the camera, the best of friends. Then the pictures stopped abruptly. There were no more—just empty pages. What did it mean? Clearly Sean had lied when he had denied that he had known Dave well—the pictures spanned a couple of years. And Dave had never, ever mentioned Sean's name—she was sure.

What had come between them? A woman? She searched back through the photographs, but though there were plenty of pretty girls, perched on a knee or held in a casual hug, none appeared regularly enough to suggest that there had been anyone special. And somehow neither seemed to be the type to quarrel so fiercely over a woman. There was also the strange hostility of Joshua and Martha—surely they wouldn't feel so strongly partisan if it had just been one of the squalls of young love?

Money, then? But again, neither seemed the sort to take money that seriously. Drugs? Had someone introduced the rich kids' folly, cocaine? But that would be more likely to unite Sean and Dave, not divide them. Serious divers took care of their bodies, and didn't abuse them with smoking or alcohol—or drugs.

She realised that she was moving into the realms of the bizarre, and shook her head impatiently. Suddenly she heard footsteps, and looked up with a guilty start as Martha appeared in the doorway. 'Oh, I ... couldn't resist looking at these old photos,' she said quickly, showing her the oldest album. 'Who are these people?'

Martha's expression was wary, 'They's a bunch of old bootleggers Mr Nat used to know,' she replied. 'You can ask him about them, I'm going to get him up now. He likes to talk about the old times. He don't get too many visitors no more, 'cept for Mr Sean. He done outlived all his friends.' She smiled broadly, but then remembered herself; the smile wavered and faded, and she stomped back down the hall.

A few minutes later she wheeled the old man, refreshed from his nap, out on to the verandah, and Kate eagerly brought the albums and put them on the low glass table in front of him. Martha brought them iced coffee, and settled down in a rocking-chair a few feet away and picked up some straw-plaiting.

For the rest of the afternoon, Kate listened spellbound as old Nat told her incredible tales of the prohibition era, of outwitting coastguards and wheeling and dealing with greedy suppliers and ruthless competitors.

Sean found them there when he returned several hours later. His grandfather shot him a penetrating glance. 'And where have you been?' he demanded sharply.

'Down to Deadman's Rock,' Sean answered, unruffled. 'I wanted to see if there were any more coins to be found around that old wreck.' He tossed a handful of worn silver discs on the table.

'Ah!' cried Nat, picking one up and handing it to Kate. 'Spanish silver. That's another part of our bloodthirsty history. Plundering the ships that ran aground out there on the sandbank. And if they didn't run aground of their own accord—well, sometimes we'd give them a little help.' His eyes were dancing points of mischief. 'My great-grandfather, William McGregor, led a gang that took twenty ships in three months,' he added proudly. 'Of course, we're directly descended from Robert McGregor, the pirate. Sailed with Captain Woodes Rogers, and turned respectable with him when he was made Royal Governor.'

'You gonna sit there talking all night, or you gonna come in for your chow?' came Martha's scolding voice behind them.

'Ah, yes,' beamed Nat, 'I've worked up quite an appetite with all this talking. Come on, boy,' he added sharply to Sean, 'make yourself useful for once. Wheel me inside.'

Sean grinned, his expression softened as he looked down at his grandfather. 'You'd better be careful,' he advised. 'Kate will think you're a thoroughly cantankerous old man.'

'I'd think nothing of the sort!' she protested quickly.

'Of course I am,' declared Nat with wicked glee. 'I'm entitled to be. I'm ninety-three years old. Outlived 'em all—and I'm not finished yet, not by a long chalk!'

The food was as delicious as at lunch. Both Sean and his grandfather regaled Kate with tales of Bahamian history, and their ancestors' part in it—usually a maverick part. Afterwards they went out on to the front porch again, and in the stillness of the night the swashbuckling stories were marvellously romantic.

A hurricane lamp flickered on the low table between them, casting dramatic shadows over their faces, and Kate's eyes drifted again and again to Sean's stone-carved profile. There was a remarkable likeness between the hard-boned features of the two men, and she could imagine that likeness being passed down through generation after generation of McGregor men, from that first ruthless buccaneer, Robert McGregor. She could see Sean in that role so easily, and smiled at herself in the darkness for her own foolish imaginings.

Martha came after a while, and insisted that the old man should go to bed. He grumbled, but gave way, and Kate kissed him affectionately on his paper-thin cheek, and bade him a fond good night.

As she watched Martha wheel the chair into the house she felt a warm shiver run through her at the thought of sitting out there alone with Sean in the quiet darkness. She glanced at him, but he seemed totally oblivious to any tension in the air, lounging back in a cane armchair, his long legs stretched in front of him.

As Kate sat down again opposite him, he coolly resumed the story he had been telling, as if there had never been anything between them. She listened to his

deep, soft voice, hardly hearing the words, her mind
filled with memories so vivid that her pulse began to
race and her cheeks were faintly pink beneath her tan.
That hungry ache gnawed at her—he was so close, she
could just reach out and touch him, let him draw her
into his arms . . .

The sky was drifted with dark, mysterious clouds,
moving high and fast across the face of the stars. The
silence around them was woven with sounds—the
whisper of the sea over the coral shallows, the rustle of
the breeze in the high heads of the jacarandas and
coco-plums, the night-song of the tree-frogs. The
flame of the lamp puttered in its glass dome, giving off
a strangely homely smell that mingled with the aroma
of the mosquito coils that kept the insects away. And
beyond that, drifting hauntingly on the night air, was
the sweet perfume of the flowering shrubs that
surrounded the house.

Kate sat quietly, watching Sean, listening to the
sound of his voice. The sleeves of his check shirt were
folded back over his strong wrists, and his hands
moved occasionally as he talked, illustrating the
action. Sometimes he would glance at her, his eyes
smiling as he spun tales of the daring adventures of his
ancestors, defying the authorities or the elemental
forces of nature.

Almost consciously she was making a memory,
etching every detail of this beautiful, bittersweet
evening into her heart, so that she would never forget
it.

It was very late when Martha appeared in the
doorway to ask if they would like another cup of coffee

before they went to bed. She was wearing a pink housecoat and well-worn slippers, and her tone hinted strongly that she had come out deliberately to remind them of the time.

'Is it that late?' remarked Sean, glancing at his watch. 'Don't you bother, Martha. I'll make it. Would you like some, Kate?'

'Oh . . . yes, please,' she managed to say, reluctant to be drawn back to reality.

'All right,' said Martha grumpily. 'But don't you go making a mess in my kitchen.' Her tone was scolding, but she beamed up at Sean fondly as he towered over her.

'I wouldn't dare,' he returned teasingly, and dropped an affectionate kiss on her forehead. 'Good night, Martha.'

'Good night, Mr Sean,' she answered gruffly.

'Good night,' added Kate hopefully.

Martha looked at her warily, but then with reluctance allowed herself to thaw a little. 'Good night, Miz Kate,' she murmured, and then vanished into the darkness of the house.

Kate sat back, and closed her eyes, a strange melancholy contracting her heart. All the differing images of Sean were coming together into a complex whole. She remembered the way he had guarded her on their dives together, the way he had killed the shark that had attacked them. He was the sort of man a woman could easily find herself coming to depend on.

And then there was that smiling warmth he reserved for those favoured few who enjoyed his affection and trust. He had never looked at her like that. For one of those smiles she would do almost anything . . .

The rich aroma of coffee drifted to her nostrils, and she opened her eyes as Sean came back on to the porch with two steaming mugs, which he set down on the table between them, next to the pile of photograph albums. Without giving herself time to plan what she was going to say, she picked up the one that held the pictures of Dave, and opened it.

'I found this when I was looking at the old photographs,' she began, her voice taut, her heart pounding painfully. She couldn't read the expression in his eyes. 'I didn't mean to pry,' she added nervously. 'I just wanted to look at the old pictures, and this album was on top. I only glanced at it to see what was in it.'

'Only glanced?' he repeated coldly.

'Well, naturally, when I saw the pictures of Dave, I looked again,' she said. She didn't even know why she was lying—it was so transparent.

'Naturally,' he sneered.

'There are a lot of them,' she rushed on, turning the pages with a trembling hand. 'You were friends once, weren't you?'

'No.'

'But . . .'

'I said we weren't friends,' he snarled, the cold fury in his voice freezing her bones. 'Dave Taylor didn't know the meaning of the word.'

'Why did you quarrel?' she asked tensely. 'What happened? Please tell me.'

For a long moment their eyes held in the flickering

glow of the oil-lamp, and then abruptly he stood up. 'Your room is at the end of the passage, on the left,' he rapped brusquely. 'Good night.'

He turned and walked away, vanishing into the shadows beneath the trees. She stared after him with wide, stricken eyes, her mind empty, her body numb. An icy chasm yawned between them, and she didn't know how to cross it.

After a while she found the strength to get up and go in search of the room she had been allotted. The house was very quiet. She could hear Nat McGregor's harsh breathing behind one door, Martha's soft snores behind another. She found the door at the end of the corridor, and opened it.

It was a small but pretty room with an old-fashioned oak bedstead covered with a hand-made patchwork quilt of sunny yellow shades. There was a rag-rug on the polished floor, and a charmingly ugly old porcelain sink in one corner.

She took off her clothes, and washed out her bikini, knowing that it would be dry by morning. Then she slipped naked between the cool cotton sheets, and lay on her back, staring up at the shadowy ceiling.

The ache in her body was almost unbearable. She hugged the pillow, but she could find no peace. She felt as if she were being torn in half. Once she had been sure that she could never love anyone as much as she had loved Dave—but now, like the rising sun, Sean had filled her whole horizon, dimming her memories.

She heard Sean return, heard him moving around quietly in the room next to hers. Heard the creak of the bed as he lay down. So close—just a few steps away.

The touch of the sheets against her bare skin was like a caress, and she turned her face into the pillow to stifle a moan of pain.

With sudden, bewildering clarity she realised that she was in love with him, beyond all doubt or question. None of the arguments she could put forward against it could convince her crazy heart. That he was a confirmed cynic, who treated women like playthings; that he was a millionaire who could buy out her father's small travel business fifty times over; that he lived in a sleazy waterfront bar that frightened the life out of her. Even that unreconciled quarrel with Dave. None of it mattered.

And now that she had made this earth-shattering discovery, she asked herself bitterly, what could she do about it? It certainly wasn't love he was offering in return. If she went to him now, accepted his terms, what would happen? Probably he would just take her coldly and then send her away, just another one-night stand. And if he did, how would she face tomorrow? She hugged the pillow, and soaked it with her tears.

They left soon after breakfast. Kate bid farewell to Sean's grandfather with regret, smiling wistfully when he expressed a hope that she would visit him again. 'I would like to,' she said sincerely, 'but when this trip is over, I'll be going straight back to England, and I doubt if I'll be able to afford to come back to the Bahamas for a long time.'

'Oh, well,' the old man sighed. 'Remember us well, then. Good memories chase out the bad.'

She looked at him, startled by the unexpected

allusion to the past. But Sean interceded, shaking his grandfather's thin hand and promising to be back in a couple of weeks.

'That's right,' nodded Nat comfortably. 'And don't you go dropping the price too much on those package bookings at Cable Beach.'

'Am I likely to?' queried Sean.

'No. I taught you well, and you're a McGregor—and that means you're no fool,' declared Nat belligerently. 'Off you go now. And watch out for the weather.'

Kate glanced up in surprise at the flawless blue sky. 'But it's going to be a lovely day,' she protested.

'Oh, I daresay it will,' the old man nodded sagely, 'but that's no guarantee tomorrow will be the same. I wouldn't be surprised if there's trouble brewing out there over the ocean somewhere.'

Sean took the warning seriously. 'No problem,' he assured him. 'We'll be out of the coral bank at the first sign of trouble.'

Kate glanced back as they walked down the path, and waved to the pair watching from the verandah. The old man lifted his frail hand and waved back, and after a moment's hesitation Martha, standing behind his wheelchair like a stern guardian angel, lifted a hand and waved too in cautious friendliness.

Then a bend in the path hid them from view, and in a few minutes they were back on the beach, where the dinghy waited where they had left it the day before. There was silence between them as they rode back to the yacht marina, and tied up alongside the *Barracuda*.

Josh and his father were already aboard, and Josh leaned over the rail to help her aboard. 'You had a nice weekend, Miz Kate?' he asked cheerfully.

'Yes, thank you, Josh,' she answered with a warm smile. 'We've been round to see Mr McGregor.'

She caught a swift, hostile glare from old Joshua before he turned away and went below decks, and a brief, wordless exchange between the two younger men. Oh, damn them all! she thought crossly. She was sick of all these mysterious undercurrents. From now on she was going to keep things strictly business. Her mouth twisted in a small smile of bitter self-mockery as she went down to her cabin. How many times had she told herself that? And every time she had weakened.

She picked up the photo of Dave, and sat cross-legged on her bunk, staring at it bleakly. It was strange how, in so short a time, the image had come to mean something so different. Not less—just different. The pain had gone, and with it—to some extent—the guilt.

She recognised now that if it had been the other way round, if she had been the one killed, she wouldn't have wanted Dave to cloister himself and never fall in love again. If only it could have been someone other than Sean McGregor who had brought about the change! The rest of the trip was going to be extremely difficult to say the least.

With a sigh, she put down the photograph and went back up on deck as Joshua was casting off from the quayside, and she stood by the rail watching as Wrecker's Cay slowly shrank and disappeared from sight. She gazed bleakly out at the empty horizon. The

island might never have existed. That evening
dancing in Sean's arms, the frenzy of those moments
on the beach, might have been no more than the
dreams of her fevered imagination.

By midday they were back at the coral bank,
weaving cautiously into the labyrinth with the sun
almost overhead. Kate could not imagine how Sean
could tell one channel from another, but he seemed to
know exactly where he was. She was not at all
surprised when she spotted one of the red marker
buoys that they had not retrieved after the shark
attack.

They passed that reef, and wound further into the
treacherous maze. They dropped anchor in the lee of
another half-moon reef. The scenery was breathtak-
ingly beautiful: the mauve and green masses of the
coral gardens alternated with the sapphire blue of the
open water. Though they were at least five miles from
the nearest land, several pretty butterflies and small
birds had taken a brief rest on the superstructure of the
boat.

'We'll dive right away.' She turned quickly as Sean
climbed down from the flying-bridge. 'While the sun's
still high,' he went on impersonally. 'Forty-five
minutes should be enough to take a look along the reef,
and then we can decide where we want to start.'

'Fine,' she responded, pleased by the cool tone of
her voice. 'I'll go and get suited-up.'

The reef wall was very steep, and thickly wooded
with branching bushes of golden acroporian coral that
masked any contours that might be there. They finned
slowly along, ten feet from the coral cliff, searching for

patterns. The reef seemed to be honeycombed with cracks and gaping holes at its base—at least, part of it was.

Kate looked more closely, her heart beginning to beat a little faster as she realised that she was looking at a tumbled mass of wooden planks, thickly encrusted with coral. Instinctively she turned to Sean, her eyes shining behind the perspex window of her face-mask. He nodded, giving her the 'okay' sign, and they swam in closer.

Now Kate could distinguish the outline of a cannon. Only the end of the muzzle was visible—it was the unnatural regularity of the coral outcrop that gave her the clue. Sean marked it with one of the inflatable red buoys, and she moved on along the reef, carefully examining every intriguing shape.

She knew that there were only seven cannon aboard the *Belle Étoile*—Philippe de Mercort had relied on speed and manoeuvrability to run up close to the clumsy treasure ships, close enough to sling up the grappling irons so that the pirates—expert seamen all and agile as cats—could swarm up the ropes and engage in their swift and bloody battle.

She had identified three more cannon, all iron breech-loaders of the type know as demi-slings, before Sean touched her arm to remind her that it was time to return to the surface. She nodded reluctantly, and began to fin upwards, reminding herself firmly to go slowly and breathe out evenly as she went.

She rose obliquely through the water, and surfaced only a few yards from the *Barracuda*. 'We've found it,

Josh!' she cried, waving excitedly. 'Oh, I can hardly believe it!'

'Can't you?' enquired Sean sardonically as he surfaced close beside her. 'I thought you had no doubts?'

She caught the cynical gleam in his eyes, and her happiness turned at once to defensive anger. 'I never doubted that it was there,' she countered frostily. 'I just didn't think we'd find it so quickly.'

'We were lucky,' he conceded as he swung himself up on to the swim-platform and turned to give her a hand up.

'So it seems,' she responded, ignoring his assistance as she climbed the ladder to the aft-deck. Josh helped her out of her diving-gear, and wrapped in a towel she sat down to drink her hot chocolate.

The sea water trickling out of her hair was a blessed disguise for the tears that were welling from the corners of her eyes. Now that they had found the wreck, it would be a matter of only a few days before it was time to return to Nassau. Some photographs, some measuring and mapping, a little salvaging of the small, movable bits of wreckage—it would not take long. And then it would be all over, she would be going back to England, and she would never see Sean again.

'You're supposed to be pleased about it.' Kate looked up in shock, wondering how he could have read her thoughts. 'You've found your precious wreck. Now you can prove what a super-hero Dave was.'

She glared up at him, stung by his cold cynicism. 'Of course I'm pleased,' she retaliated swiftly. 'I was just wishing he could have been here himself to share it.'

'Not on my boat,' muttered Sean.

Kate slanted him an angry glance. 'Why didn't you like him?' she demanded in a voice sharp with tension. 'Why won't you tell me why you quarrelled?'

Suddenly he was leaning over her, tilting her face up to his. 'Because I wouldn't want to shatter your illusions, little Kate,' he sneered softly.

'I don't think I'd believe anything you told me about him, anyway,' she told him, returning his contempt.

'Then I'd be wasting my breath, wouldn't I?'

She jerked her head away from him impatiently. He was quite invulnerable to her poison darts—was there no chink in his armour?

He moved away from her to sit on the far side of the deck. 'So what happens now?' he enquired in a sardonic drawl.

With an effort of will she pulled herself together. 'I'd like to have a look inside the wreck,' she said, 'and then I can start taking pictures of it.'

'You can develop your photographs here on board if you like,' he told her. 'The galley can double as a dark-room, and we carry some basic equipment. You can't make prints, of course—it would be impossible under these conditions.'

She nodded. 'It doesn't matter. I want to make transparencies anyway—they're better for publication.' Kate hesitated for a moment. 'I'd like to be able to get in touch with Mr Thompson, and let him know that we've found her,' she added.

'You can use the ship-to-shore. You'd better book a call this afternoon.'

'Thank you. Do you know how much it would cost

to call London from here?'

He shrugged indifferently. 'Forget it.'

'I want to pay you,' she insisted.

'I said forget it,' he repeated sharply. 'Just don't mention my name, okay? I don't want to be besieged by a hoard of amateur treasure-hunters wanting me to help them get themselves killed.'

'Very well,' she said tightly. 'I'll book the call now, before I have my shower.'

Mr Thompson was delighted. 'Good girl,' he approved. 'We'll do a six-page spread. Lots of photographs. Can you do that?'

'Yes, I can,' she assured him, careful to speak very distinctly so that he could catch every word. 'Do you want me to write something to go with the pictures?'

She waited the long seconds until Mr Thompson's voice came back through the white noise on the long-distance line. 'Of course. Let me have a couple of thousand words. We can always clip it if we want more space for the prints. How soon will you be back in England?'

'About a week,' she answered. 'I'll call you as soon as I get back.'

'Fine. I'll look forward to seeing you—and the photographs. Goodbye.'

'Goodbye . . .' But the connection had already gone dead. She put down the headset of the radio-telephone with a small sigh, and leaned back in the navigator's seat, rubbing her hands over her face. She felt wrung out, exhausted.

One more week, and then she would never see Sean

again. Perhaps it was just as well. There seemed to be little hope of reconciling the conflict in her heart. Sean was colder towards her than ever, and she knew now that his quarrel with Dave must have been about something quite important. She felt as if she were being called on to take sides in a dispute she didn't even understand.

CHAPTER NINE

THE next day Kate undertook a more detailed
examination of the site, exploring carefully the maze
of caverns beneath the tumbled deck-planks. She wore
a diving-helmet, with a light shining out from the
middle of her forehead; a fine nylon line connected
her to Sean who waited outside on guard.

Inside she found the remaining cannon, which had
been on the other side of the deck, and finally another
large mass of coral that positively demanded attention. As she chipped away at the encrusting coral, she
knew that she had found the anchor: 'iron anchor of
French design, *circa* 1700'. How strange to think that
Dave had been at this very spot, seen what she was
seeing now, all those years ago.

A double tug on the line reminded her that she had
only five minutes bottom-time left. Pausing only to
collect a couple of interesting lumps of coral from the
debris and sand at the bottom, she followed the line
back through the labyrinth to emerge with relief into
the open water.

She surfaced carefully, using her buoyancy-jacket to
counteract the extra weight of her finds. Sean rose
beside her, ready to help her if she needed it. But
within a few minutes she was safely back on the aft-
deck, and Josh was bubbling with excitement,
convinced that she had found sunken treasure.

'I doubt it, Josh,' she told him, laughing. 'If there's anything in those clumps, it'll be no more than pewter or bronze. Get me a bowl and some vinegar and we'll have a look.'

To Josh's disappointment she proved to be right. One clump yielded a cheap pewter drinking-cup, and the other an iron dagger handle, almost rusted away.

On their second dive of the day, Kate took Dave's underwater camera down with her to the wreck-site. It was far from easy to take photographs at that depth— the water distorted size and distance, and absorbed most of the light. She took a light-reading, and handed one of the two powerful strobe-flashes to Sean, indicating that he should direct it on to her subject— one of the cannon—from a little above her left shoulder. He picked up her instructions instantly, though he was still constantly alert to any dangers in the water around them.

She took several shots of the cannon, bracketing the optimum f-setting to get a range of results, and then moved on to the next subject she had chosen. She shot several cartridges of film, photographing every detail of the site to build up a composite mosaic.

When their time was up they surfaced together and swam back to the *Barracuda*. 'That was good,' remarked Kate as she paused on the swim-platform to take off her flippers. 'I just hope they come out all right.'

'You can develop them after lunch,' he suggested.

Kate glanced at him, wishing she could detect just a hint of warmth in his impersonal tone. But there was none. Already the co-operation that existed between them below the water had vanished, and that invisible barrier had risen again. There was a heavy sadness in her heart as she passed the precious camera up to Josh, and climbed the ladder to the aft-deck.

'Thanks, Josh,' she said as he took her diving-gear to rinse it for her. 'Leave the camera—I'll deal with that.'

After lunch, Sean pulled a crate of photographic equipment from one of the underseat lockers in the saloon, and carried it through to the galley for her. 'I think you'll find everything you need in here,' he told her. 'Chemicals, tanks, thermometers, whatever . . . With the doors closed, the light-seal is pretty good. Don't worry about ventilation—the air-conditioning can deal with that.'

She watched as he taped black card across the port-holes, and changed the light-bulb for an orange safe-light. 'You certainly have everything you could want aboard this boat,' she said, striving to hide her nervousness at being so close to him in the confined space of the galley. The dimness lent a dangerous intimacy to the atmosphere, and she couldn't stop herself edging uneasily away from him, certain that he could hear the unsteady pounding of her heart.

'One of the advantages of being rich,' he drawled, 'is that you can afford to buy anything you want.'

'How pleasant for you,' she countered caustically, stung by his sardonic manner.

'It is.'

'You can't buy anything that really matters, though,' she added, deliberately needling him. 'You can't buy friendship—or love.'

'Maybe not,' he agreed mockingly. 'But you can buy the pretence—and after a while you can get so you don't notice the difference.'

She stared at him bleakly. 'Why are you always so cynical?'

Suddenly he had trapped her against the sink-unit, his sneering face inches above hers. 'Maybe life's taught me a few tough lessons you've yet to learn, little Kate.'

She twisted away from him, putting her hands up against his chest in an instinctive gesture of defence. 'I hope I never have to learn,' she hissed 'Not if it would make me as disagreeable as you.'

She could feel the tension of anger in him, and closed her eyes, expecting a storm. But abruptly he turned away, leaving her staring at the door as he closed it firmly behind him.

Pulling herself together with difficulty, she forced herself to turn her full attention to the job in hand. The chemicals were powdered, and needed very careful mixing, and she had increased the film-speed a little to make up for the amount of light absorbed by the water, so she had to adjust the time she allowed in some of the developing stages.

It was a very precise process, requiring all her concentration. She worked with the deftness of experience—Dave had found this part of the work tedious, and had left it to her as soon as he had been satisfied of her competence—and for a while she was able to put all other thoughts from her mind. She even found herself singing as she worked—one of the infectiously simple goombay songs she had heard on Josh's radio.

The strips of colour transparencies were still fogged when she had finished developing them—they wouldn't clear until they were dry. She packed the equipment away, and carried the film strips through to hang them up safely in her own bathroom. Then she went back up on deck to write up her notes.

It had been a very hot day, and Kate was glad of the cool breeze that sprang up towards evening. The sunset was magnificent, washing the sky with crimson and purple. They dined as usual on the aft-deck, alone. The silence lay heavy around them, and neither of them chose to speak more than the merest politeness demanded.

Kate went to bed early, but she didn't sleep well. Images of diving among the coral wove patterns in her mind, and her ears echoed with the memories of Sean's words—'You can buy the pretence.' And again she remembered what he had said before: 'If someone is going to stick a knife in my back, it'll be the sort I can see.'

What had happened all those years ago to make him so hard, so cynical? And would there ever be a way back for him—back to the human race? A small, sad tear trickled down her cheek. If ever there was, she would not be there to share it. She of all people, because she was Dave Taylor's wife.

She picked up the photograph, and studied it intently. It must have been some kind of crazy misunderstanding, she was sure. But it was too late to put it right now, even if she knew how. Far too late.

She turned over, punching the pillow into a more comfortable shape, and tried to make herself fall asleep.

Next morning she finished photographing the exterior of the wreck-site. She took her time—she was in no hurry to venture inside those claustrophobic caverns again. She could understand why Sean had described it as dangerous—to an inexperienced diver it could be a death-trap. It was a relief to escape to open water again, and over lunch she was tense, knowing that she had to go back into the wreck that afternoon to finish the photographs.

But she hid her feelings from Sean, fearing his mockery more than she feared the dive. After lunch she settled herself on the aft-deck, trying to draw a sketch-map of the wreck-site; but it was difficult to visualise what lay beneath the water.

The weather was even hotter, and by the time three o'clock came Kate was glad to go back into the water, even if it did mean facing the dive into the labyrinth of the *Belle Étoile*. She worked steadily, and managed to finish all the photographs she wanted to take before it was time to surface. After her shower she developed all the remaining film strips, and hung them up with the others.

When she went back up on deck, she found that the sea had changed, losing its blue-green clarity. It was flecked with leaden grey, and by late afternoon choppy little waves were breaking up its tranquil surface. The radio was tuned to a local hot-gospel station, and the fervent tones of a hell-fire preacher were regularly interspersed with weather reports.

There was a hurricane brewing out over the Atlantic; the forecasts predicted that it wouldn't come too close to the Bahamas—but a hurricane could be a peculiarly contrary beast. There was no cooling breeze that evening, and the sunset was almost too beautiful—flaming shards of amber light slicing through massive banks of blue-black clouds. Kate gazed at it, her breath stilled in wonder.

When at last she turned away, she saw Sean standing in the doorway of the saloon, watching the sunset too. 'Wasn't it lovely?' she remarked, trying to smile.

'Very nice. It's going to be quite a storm.'

'Is it safe for us to stay here?' she asked.

His eyes glinted with mockery. 'I'm not risking my boat for your damned wreck,' he told her. 'I've marked the channel. If the weather gets too bad we'll run for Nassau.'

'Why not a nearer port?'

'I don't want to be holed up on Andros for days on end,' he answered brusquely. 'You've got your photographs. Another day or so should be all you need to finish the job.'

Kate's heart twisted in pain. Just another day or so . . . and then she would be back in Nassau, catching a plane back to England. And she would never see Sean again. Suddenly all she wanted to do was reach out and touch him—but he had already gone back into the saloon, and she could only follow him, her face a mask to hide her feelings as she sat down opposite him at the dinner table.

The boat was moving on that long, slow swell, characteristic of an impending hurricane. There was a tense expectancy in the air, as if a vast elemental orchestra were tuning up. The curtain would rise within the next twenty-four hours.

But whether the *Barracuda* rode out the fringes of the storm or was forced to run before it, her own small drama was almost over. Josh's skill with grouper cutlets was wasted on her palate. She could eat little, and pushed aside her plate with a dismal little sigh.

'I'm not very hungry,' she explained to Sean when he glanced at her questioningly. 'It's this heat.'

He nodded without saying anything. Kate sat back, and half-turned in her seat to gaze up at the night sky, a study in inky shades of darkness. High, fast clouds raced across the face of the stars, and the moon was a sickly yellow. It was going to be a hot, troubled night.

The ranting tones of the evangelist on the radio made Kate's head ache. 'Isn't there anything else on?' she demanded impatiently. Sean shook his head. 'Oh, there must be!' she snapped, getting up to go over to the radio.

'Leave it alone,' ordered Sean flatly. 'We've got to hear the weather reports.'

'Oh, damn!' She sat down again, a frown creasing her brow. She felt imprisoned by the heat, wishing something explosive would happen to clear the tension in her head. Sean sat reading a magazine, apparently impervious to the sultry atmosphere. What would shake him, she wondered recklessly. What would turn on that wild, dangerous anger? Her fevered imagination begain to spin a scene of torrid drama, in which he carried her off to his cabin, taking no heed of her struggles.

But when she glanced cautiously towards him, her courage to speak the opening lines of the script failed, and instead she said thinly, 'I think I'll go and lie down on my bunk.'

Sean glanced at his watch. 'It's early yet,' he remarked indifferently.

'I know. But I'm bored. I might read for a bit.' She went down to her cabin and took off all her clothes. Another quick shower cooled her a little, and she lay down on top of the bedcover and closed her eyes.

There was a kind of desperation in her heart. Tonight was their last night on the boat—she felt it with a brooding certainty. And she wanted to spend it with Sean, wanted to lie naked in his arms, feel his flesh against hers. Just one night. To hell with tomorrow. She wanted him, wanted to feel him need her, wanted to find out what it would be like on the other side of that great chasm that divided them. Would they maybe . . . just maybe . . . find that there could be a tomorrow for them after all?

No. She shook her head brusquely. There could be no tomorrow. She must not let herself think like that. The fires inside her raged hot enough, without her adding the fuel of her wild fantasies. One night with Sean would be a night of paradise, but the pain that would follow would take a long, long time to fade.

But the long, sultry night alone in her bunk was a purgatory itself. Her spirits were sinking with the mercury in the barometer, and she barely slept. From time to time she could hear Sean or old Joshua moving about on deck, checking the anchors.

It was reassuring to know that, if the storm reached them, she would be in safe hands. Sean would never take an unnecessary risk with the *Barracuda*—he knew exactly where the narrow divide lay between courage and foolhardiness. And he had no need for acts of bravado—he had nothing to prove. As she sank at last into restless dreams her memories went with her, haunting her through the long watches of the night.

At long last the darkness began to pale. Kate knelt up on the bunk to look out of the port-hole; the sunrise was obscured by low-lying clouds along the horizon, and above them great beams of pale gold light shafted out across the purple sky. Already it was uncomfortably warm.

She had a cool shower, blessing the *Barracuda's* luxurious distillation plant that gave her such free use of fresh water, and then, dressed as lightly as possible in shorts and a loose cotton top she went up on deck. She could only stand and gaze in awestruck wonder at the massive inky clouds that seemed to roll up almost out of the sea.

Two hundred miles away, near the eye of the storm, the winds would be devastating. Out here on its very fringes the sea was a brooding grey, and the *Barracuda* was rocking quite strongly on her anchor chains.

'Can we dive today?' she asked Sean as he walked down the side deck from the bows.

'If it gets no worse,' he responded briefly.

She hesitated for a moment, reluctant to broach the

subject of money with him again. But it had to be sorted out. 'Perhaps ... perhaps we might as well settle up now. If you could just tell me how much I owe you?'

He turned to her in mocking enquiry. 'I beg your pardon?'

'My bill. For chartering the boat and ... and everything. Will it be all right if I pay by cheque?'

He gave a sardonic laugh. 'Oh, you're offering to pay me?' he taunted. 'Let me see, what should I charge for dancing with you? And flattering your feminine ego with kisses? Oh, and making love to you on the beach—that should be worth a few dollars—less a discount for not finishing the job, of course.'

She stared at him, bewildered and hurt by his acid words. 'Stop it,' she begged. 'Why are you saying things like that?'

'You raised the subject of money.'

She blinked back the tears that were stinging her eyes. 'Look,' she managed to say, 'we had an agreement that I would charter your boat at the standard rate. Anything that ... that happened between us is beside the point.'

'But I'm not in the charter business,' he reminded her.

'I know.' She looked down at her hands, twisting in her lap. 'I'm sorry I made that mistake. But I still want to pay.'

'I don't need your money. This whole trip's cost less than I might lose on the turn of one card.'

'That doesn't make any difference,' she insisted with dignity. 'It might be only pocket money to you, but it's important to me.'

His lip curled in an unpleasant sneer. 'Oh, I forgot. You're the girl who isn't impressed by money. Forgive me. Such integrity is so rare a quality.'

'Have you ever stopped to consider that maybe people would like to be friends with you, but you never give them the chance?' she suggested bitterly.

'Oh, yes?' His tone was coldly mocking. 'What about you, little Kate? Would you like to be my friend?' Before she could defend herself, he had dragged her to her feet, and pinned her back against the wall of the saloon cabin. 'What sort of friend would you be?' he demanded harshly. 'What sort of lover? Would you be as loyal to me as you are to your dear, departed husband?'

She closed her eyes, too weak to fight him. 'You want me, don't you, Kate?' His hand roved down over her body with rough gentleness. 'Go on, admit it,' he persisted. 'I can feel the way you're responding.'

Tears trickled down her face as the inevitable wave of desire his touch aroused clashed head on with the pain his cold contempt was searing into her heart. He drew her into his arms, but his voice was like cold steel. 'So how about it, little Kate? Shall we go to bed? How would you like to make love to a murderer?'

Her eyes flew open, and her heart froze in shock. He made no attempt to stop her as she backed away from him. His face was as hard as granite and so was his voice. 'So much for your mealy-mouthed platitudes,' he snarled. 'How often do you think I've seen that look in people's eyes? Friends? Oh, yes, everyone wants to be friends with a millionaire—until they hear the gossip. Then the smile becomes just a little too fixed—you know what I mean? So I think I'll stick with the miscreants and cut-throats down at the Runner, thank you. I'm one of them, and they take me for what I am.'

Kate's eyes had not left his face. She didn't know if he were telling the truth or not—her mind was numb. She just stood and stared at him. And then as if released from an evil spell she turned and ran down the steps to her own cabin.

She stood in the middle of the cabin, trembling violently. Surely it couldn't be true—he had just been trying to frighten her. Stepping into the bathroom she caught sight of herself in the mirror above the sink. Her eyes looked huge in a face that was ashen beneath her tan. Her hands were shaking, and her stomach was in knots. No, it wasn't true. She would not believe it.

She washed her face, and changed her clothes again, moving as if in a dream. The sultry heat was making her head ache, and she knew she hadn't had enough sleep. That was why she had had that strange nightmare; that was all it was—she had fallen asleep, and dreamt the whole thing.

Warily she crept back up to the saloon. She could hear Josh whistling in the galley, and old Joshua was on the aft-deck, tidying one of the underseat lockers. But there was no sign of Sean. He didn't appear until it was time to dive, and his manner was brusque and impersonal. She matched her manner to his, trying to pretend that nothing had happened. But she couldn't meet his eyes.

They both wore helmets to dive; after days of clear, tranquil waters it was unnerving to find visibility reduced to no more than twenty feet, and to have to concentrate on resisting the drag of the current.

But even so, conditions were no worse than those she had often experienced in the English Channel, and once she had got used to it she found her confidence returned. They were surveying the site, taking measurements with a marked wire line, and she noted the results on a special pad attached to her weight-belt.

Sometimes they were visible to each other only by the lights on their helmets, and it was difficult to keep the wire taut against the movement of the water, but they worked steadily and succeeded in mapping the stern half of the site. Now that she was back among the wreckage, Kate could visualise clearly again what she had seen on the first day before the fog came down to obscure the middle distance.

Back on the *Barracuda*, she began to draw a detailed diagram of the site on graph paper. Josh kept her well supplied with can after can of ice-cool sea-grape soda, and she was grateful for the air-conditioning in the saloon. But her mind was fidgeting, and her concentration poor.

Try as she might to ignore it, she couldn't forget what Sean had told her. It was a nightmare—but she hadn't dreamed it. How could it have happened? Not in cold blood, of that she was convinced. A fight, perhaps, or a car crash? And in what way had Dave been involved? She couldn't bear to think about it. Resolutely she turned her mind back to her work.

The storm was getting closer, and the heat was almost unbearable. For the umpteenth time she glanced at her watch. It was nearly half past two. At the sound of Sean's approaching footsteps she bent her head diligently over her graph paper.

'We can make one more dive,' he told her crisply. 'You'd better get ready now. I want to be out of here in an hour. This is your last chance to finish whatever you want to do—once we get to Nassau, I'm not coming back.'

Visibility down on the wreck-site was even worse—less than ten feet—and the swell was becoming strong enough to be a problem. Nevertheless they were able to measure out the for'ard half of the wreck, and glancing at her watch Kate saw that she had a few minutes left before it was time to surface. The sea was becoming rougher; bits of coral debris were avalanching down from the reef, and one of them bounced off her air-tanks with a loud clang. But she had to make the most of this last opportunity.

Touching Sean's shoulder, she signalled to him that she intended to go back inside the wreck, to look for more small artefacts to salvage. He shook his head, but she insisted, swimming down through one of the gaps before he could stop her. She had brought a net bag with her, and she worked quickly, filling it with any lumps of coral that looked as if they could conceal something of interest.

Suddenly there was a loud roar, and the next instant the cavern was collapsing around her. Instinctively she threw up her hands to protect her head, screaming silently in the watery darkness as wood and coral cascaded down. It seemed to last for hours.

At last the rumbling stopped, to be replaced by an eerie silence. Kate twisted wildly in panic, but she was trapped by one foot, and her face-mask had filled with water, blinding her. She reached out desperately for Sean, terror ripping at her heart. He was there at once, taking both her wrists in a reassuring grip, and she felt him urging her to be calm.

She was breathing too hard and too jerkily, using up her precious air too quickly, but under his influence, conveyed only through the touch of his fingers, she steadied a little. Then he moved away, and she felt the weight that was trapping her lift a little—but not enough for her to wriggle free.

Panic rose inside her again—how much air did she have left? If only she could see! Calm—she must stay calm. Sean would rescue her. She made herself hear her grandfather's quiet voice as he taught her how to clear her face-mask. Automatically she followed the instructions, blowing out hard through her nose to displace the water with air again.

Now she could see what was trapping her foot. A mass of planks, concreted together by the encrusting coral, had fallen across her ankle, and with a sick feeling she realised how easily her leg could have been crushed. The water tended to anaesthetise pain, but she could wriggle her toes still, so she was fairly sure that she wasn't badly hurt.

But a glance at her air-gauge told her that she had only a few minutes supply left in her tanks—her panic had more than doubled her rate of consumption. She touched Sean's arm and showed him the gauge. He nodded, and turned quickly back to the task of freeing her, shoving aside planks and throwing up a swirling fog of sediment.

She tried to be patient, but she could feel the drag of resistance as her air-tanks emptied, and in another moment she had to signal to Sean that she needed to share his air. His supply would be running low too, from all the activity, though he had wasted none in panic. She tried not to let herself think about what would happen if that precious air ran out before he had freed her.

He gave her his mouthpiece, and she took two good breaths, and then closing her eyes tightly to shut out her fear she let him go. She had to force herself not to hold the air in her lungs—at that depth it could cause hypoxia—and slowly she breathed out, blindly trusting that Sean would bring back the air before she drowned.

She could hear him behind her, dragging aside the concreted planks. He came back with the mouthpiece just as she was beginning to feel dizzy, his arm comfortingly around her waist as she breathed his air. She gazed up at him, wishing she could tell him all she felt—but in that wordless world she could only hope that he could read her message in her eyes.

She gave him back the mouthpiece after her second breath. A sort of quiet resignation had come to her. The seconds were ticking away, the darkness was rolling in. Suddenly the pressure against her ankle was gone, and with a convulsive jerk she twisted free, leaving her flipper behind.

Her lungs were screaming for air, but Sean was there, pushing the mouthpiece between her lips, and she took a deep, dangerous gulp. They were out of the wreck, and rising slowly from the bottom, and she clung to him helplessly as he crushed her lungs and forced her to breath out. She took a second breath, and then he took the air-supply back for himself.

But it didn't matter. She could see the pearlescent glow of the surface, only a few feet away, and then she was looking up into a cloud-strewn sky that she had thought she would never see again. Completely overcome, she began to cry.

Sean jettisoned both their weight-belts and air-tanks, and made her drop the net bag, to which she was still clinging almost convulsively. Then he began to tow her towards the boat. Josh had realised that something was wrong, and had climbed down the ladder to the swim-platform to help Sean get her out of the water, and old Joshua was leaning over the transom.

Somehow they manhandled her aboard, and laid her down gently on the aft-deck. Her ankle was beginning to throb with pain, and her head felt light. Sean helped her take off her wetsuit, and then he knelt beside her to examine her injury with gentle care.

'I think it's only bruised,' he said. 'I'll get a doctor to have a look at it when we get back to Nassau.' He stood up, and began stripping off his own wetsuit. 'You'd better lie down for a while,' he went on. 'Can you stand?'

'I . . . I don't know.' All she wanted was to feel his arms around her again. Why think about tomorrow? Without Sean, she might not have lived to see tomorrow. She didn't care what he'd done. She didn't care about anything but the aching hunger inside her. As he helped her to her feet she leaned against him, exaggerating her weakness as an excuse.

He frowned anxiously. 'Perhaps I'd better carry you,' he said. As he scooped her up in his arms she let her head rest against his shoulder, and her heart began to race. 'Weigh the anchors and take us out of here, Joshua,' he called as he manoeuvred her through the saloon door and down to her cabin.

As he set her on her feet she kept her arms around his neck. 'I'd like to have a shower,' she said softly. 'I don't like letting the sea-water dry in my hair.' As he hestitated she added daringly, 'Will you help me? Just in case I slip?'

She felt him tense, and peeped up cautiously through her lashes. His mouth had compressed into a hard line. Without a word he picked her up again and carried her into the shower, and set her on her feet, holding her firmly away from him.

The warm water ran down over their bodies, and Kate watched in fascination as it trickled in tiny rivulets through the rough smattering of hair across his wide, bronzed chest. Almost unconsciously she put up her hand, and began to trace a path through the curling patterns. She could feel his heart-beat, fast and strong beneath her fingertips.

He caught her hand and snatched it away, so she lifted the other, and he caught that too. 'Stop it, Kate,' he warned harshly. She gazed up at him, and a small smile of certainty curved her mouth. He grasped her shoulders, and shook her roughly. 'For Christ's sake, stop it.'

She wrapped her arms around his waist, and pressed her whole body against his, burying her face against the hard wall of his chest, her hungry mouth savouring the taste of his flesh. There was no mistaking the dangerous tension of male arousal in him, and she marvelled that he could still control himself at all.

'Kate!' His voice had thickened huskily. 'You don't know what you're doing. You must be in shock.'

She looked up at him, her dark eyes glittering. 'Oh, no, I'm not,' she whispered hotly.

For one tense moment she thought he would break away from her. But then with a sudden savage fierceness he pushed her back against the tiled wall, one hand imprisoning her, as with a swift movement he peeled off her wet swimsuit and let it drop around her feet. She surrendered without restraint to his mastering strength as he half-dragged her from the shower and threw her down across one of the bunks, to take her with an urgent demand that would brook no resistance.

The *Barracuda* was running before the storm, her powerful engines throbbing as she surged through the water at high speed, her bows plunging into the troughs between the waves.

CHAPTER TEN

As Sean's harsh breathing returned slowly to normal he shifted his weight from Kate, and lay beside her, looking down into her face, his eyes defended against all her efforts to read what was in his mind. At last he said gruffly, 'I'm not going to apologise. That was your own fault.'

'I know,' she answered steadily. She must not cry—not until he had gone.

He sighed, and looked away from her, and then back, reluctantly. 'Does your ankle still hurt?' he asked.

'Not much.'

He stood up. 'You'd better rest till we get back to Nassau,' he said. 'I'll radio ahead for a doctor to come and have a look at you.' There was a gentle note in his voice now, but his kindness was only another barrier between them. He felt responsible for her because he was the skipper of the boat, and she was injured—not because he had made love to her.

He looked around for a towel, and helping her to sit up he rubbed her hair dry for her. 'Do you have a nightgown or something to put on?' he asked.

'Pyjamas,' she told him. 'Under the pillow.'

He found them, and helped her into them, and then settled her comfortably into bed. 'Go to sleep,' he said softly, and then bent over her swiftly to drop the lightest kiss on her forehead.

She fought back the instinct to reach for his hand, beg him to stay with her. She had given herself willingly, and now she had no right to make demands on him. He went out, closing the door with a firm click, and the silent tears welled up slowly, coming from deep inside her.

She had known that it would be like this, but that made it no easier to bear. She had tried to reach out across that yawning chasm he had set between himself and the rest of humanity, but she hadn't been able to touch him.

The *Barracuda* was like a living thing, surging through the water, its engines pounding with a deep, driving rhythm like the beat of a heart. Taking her back to Nassau. And yet there was something soothing in the smooth, rapid motion, and as she lay back against the pillow dark waves of sleep rolled over her, drowning her.

She woke as the steady note of the engines changed. They were coming in to Nassau harbour. It was dark, and the angry roaring of the wind told her that the hurricane had followed them home. She lay staring at the ceiling as the boat manoeuvered on the rough water, reversing into her berth with a gentle thud, and the sound of the engines died.

A few moments later there was a tap on the door. She sat up quickly, calling, 'Come in,' in a voice that betrayed all her eager anxiety.

But it was young Josh who peeped round the door, his dark eyes shaded with worry. 'You feelin' better now, Miz Kate?' he asked sympathetically.

'Yes, thank you, Josh,' she answered.

'Mista Sean said I was to pack up your things for you. He gonna carry you up to the house.'

'But I can walk,' she protested quickly.

'You'd better keep the weight off that ankle until the doctor's seen it,' came Sean's voice as he stepped into the cabin. 'Don't bother to get dressed. I'll wrap you up in one of the quilts. It isn't far.'

She didn't argue. As he folded her up in the big quilt and picked her up in his arms she felt very small and vulnerable, longing for just one word from him to let her know that he cared even a little for her. But none was forthcoming, and she felt like a thief, stealing a secret pleasure from these few precious moments he held her close.

The *Barracuda* was pitching like a rodeo-rider on the angry waves, but Sean bore her safely up on to the quayside as if she weighed nothing at all. The sky was filled with hurrying dark clouds that completely obscured the stars, and the streets were almost empty. Here and there a shutter banged, a tin can rolled or a sheet of paper sailed through the air. Odd snatches of music or conversation wafted on the wind.

Josh hurried along beside them as Sean strode up from the harbour towards the Rum Runner, and opened a wrought-iron gate at the side of the building that Kate had not noticed on her first visit. A flagged path, between riotous beds of bright hibiscus, led to a wide flight of stone steps and an elegantly porticoed front door.

Kate's eyes were already wide with surprise when

the door opened, as if they were awaited, and Maxie welcomed them into a beautiful marble hallway. 'Heavens, you poor thing!' she cried, warmly sympathetic. 'It must have been awful, being trapped like that!' She shuddered. 'I've made up the bed in the guest room like you said, Sean, and there's coffee on the stove. Are you hungry?' she added to Kate.

'A bit,' admitted Kate. 'But I don't want to put you to any trouble.'

'Oh, it ain't no trouble,' Maxie promised with a wide, friendly smile. 'There ain't many customers in tonight—the others can manage well enough without me for a while.'

Kate managed a small smile. Maxie looked senstaional—her gleaming blonde curls tumbled from a ribbon high on one side of her head, and she wore a shimmering blue jump-suit that would have been a disaster on a less perfect figure. 'Out of my league,' Kate thought ruefully. She had let herself forget about Maxie's existence these past few days, and it was embarrassing now to face her, after what had happened only hours before. She seemed to have guessed nothing—but maybe she was used to Sean being unfaithful, and had learned to take no notice.

Sean carried her up the stairs, with Josh and Maxie following. On the top floor he turned into a large bedroom, charmingly old-fashioned as if it had been furnished in the 1930s and rarely used since. Maxie hurried forward and turned back the bed-clothes, and Sean set Kate down carefully on the cool white sheets.

'Thank you,' she murmured, keeping her lashes lowered over eyes that were filled with unshed tears.

At that moment the doorbell chimed. 'That's the doctor,' said Maxie. 'He timed that well.' She hurried from the room.

Josh put Kate's bag down on the floor, and smiled at her shyly. 'I'd best be getting back to help my pappy now, Miz Kate,' he said. 'Bye-bye. Take care. Hope I sees you again before you leaves.'

'Oh, yes, of course, Josh,' she said quickly, struck by the awful finality of his words. 'I'll come and say goodbye.'

He grinned, and then he too went out, leaving her alone with Sean. It was the first time they had been alone since those devastating moments in her cabin, and she watched him covertly as he moved about the room, checking the shutters, turning on a bedside light for her. He seemed to be feeling as uncomfortable as she was, but neither of them spoke until the doctor came into the room.

Sean greeted him as an old friend. 'Tom. Thank you for coming so quickly.'

'My pleasure,' the doctor answered as the two men shook hands. 'How's the old man?'

'Very well. The arthritis is troubling him a little, but apart from that he's his usual self.'

'The old dog. He'll clock up his century yet. Now then, young lady,' he added, turning to Kate. 'What have you been up to?'

'I'm fine, really,' she insisted, 'I've just got a few bruises, that's all.'

She lifted her leg out from under the bedclothes—gingerly, because it was rather painful. Her ankle was swollen and the redness was turning a vivid purple-blue. The doctor examined it gently but thoroughly, making her wince as he manipulated the joint.

'Well, it seems you were pretty lucky,' he remarked with masterly understatement. 'You haven't broken anything, and I don't think you've even sprained it. That bruising will go down in a day or two. In the meantime, just keep it rested.' He sat on the side of the bed and took her pulse, and shone a light into her eyes. 'No bumps on the head?' he asked.

'No,' she told him. 'I ran a little short of air, but it was no problem.' She glanced swiftly up at Sean; his blue eyes were resting on her in concern, and her heart skipped so violently she was afraid the doctor might notice it. She looked away quickly.

'Well, just take it easy for a day or two, eh?' the doctor advised her. 'You can't do much else with this storm brewing,' he added as a sudden gust of wind rattled the shutters. 'It'll be keeping us all indoors for the next twenty-four hours, I reckon.' He stood up, and grinned at Sean. 'She'll be all right,' he said cheerfully. 'I shouldn't worry about her. She's tougher than she looks.'

Sean nodded. 'Good. Have you time to stop for some coffee? Or maybe something stronger?'

'I won't say no,' the doctor agreed. 'By the way, have you seen this new running back that's supposed to be signing for the Dolphins? They say he's faster . . .'

As the two men went from the room Sean glanced back at Kate, and gave her a brief smile. Her spirits soared crazily. Just for a fleeting instant, she thought she'd seen . . . she couldn't be sure . . . just a hint of some kind of special warmth.

But even as she closed her eyes to treasure the moment, Maxie came back into the room, and the tiny bubble of happiness burst. 'I've brought you some coffee, and an omelette,' she announced, setting down a tray on the bedside table. 'I hope you like it.'

Kate sat up again quickly. 'Oh, thank you. Thank you very much. It's really very kind of you, letting me stay like this.'

Maxie's warm smile flashed out. 'Oh, that's okay. It ain't no trouble at all. And anyway, it's Sean's house, not mine. I only rent the ground floor.'

Kate stared at her in blank astonishment. 'But I thought . . . ?'

'That we lived together?' enquired Maxie with devastating frankness. 'No such luck. We're just good friends, as the saying goes. We practically grew up together. My mum used to be his grandfather's cook.'

'Oh,' murmured Kate in confusion. 'I . . . I just . . .'

'Oh, I ain't saying we're like brother and sister,' Maxie amended. 'In fact, there was a time, before my second marriage . . . But I blew it, as usual. I'm a walking disaster area when it comes to men.'

Kate laughed. 'I find that hard to believe,' she said sincerely.

'It's true,' Maxie affirmed. 'I seem to bring out the rat in them. Oh, not Sean—he's been a real good friend to me, picked me up every time I got myself in a mess. When my third husband ditched me, well . . . I didn't even have a roof over my head, and I won't tell you how I was having to earn my living. When Sean found out about it, he came and fetched me back here, and gave me a respectable job, and he's putting both my kids through school—and neither of them are his, contrary to what some of the gossips will tell you.'

'Anyway,' she added cheerfully, 'I expect you're tired, and I'd better get down to the bar, though I don't reckon we'll have too many in tonight. I hope you can sleep, with this storm blowing. But at least if we get some rain it'll cool the air down a bit. It's so stuffy I can hardly breathe. Good night. See you in the morning.'

'Good night,' Kate managed to say as Maxie went out, closing the door firmly behind her. She lay back against the pillows, staring blankly at the ceiling. Maxie's words were swirling in her brain; the picture they had painted, of a gentle, generous man, matched the image that she had sometimes glimpsed so elusively behind the stony mask he chose to wear.

But now the voyage was over, and she didn't even know if he would come back to say goodbye.

Though she wasn't really hungry, she made herself eat the omelette that Maxie had brought her, and drink the coffee, and then she slid down under the covers, suddenly realising that she was still dreadfully tired, although she had already slept for several hours as the *Barracuda* had sailed home.

The wind wailed mournfully around the house, and from below she could hear faint snatches of music drifting up from the Rum Runner's bar—haunting melodies of love that tugged at her heart. She fell asleep as the first drenching shower of rain from the approaching hurricane pattered against the closed shutters.

She was deep in watery darkness, and something was holding her down. She twisted violently, trying to break free. 'Sean! Sean! Help me, please!'

'It's all right, little Kate. I'm here.' She was gathered up gently in his arms, and he stroked her hair comfortingly. 'It was just a bad dream,' he murmured soothingly. 'You're safe now. No need to cry.'

But she was sobbing painfully, clinging to him as if she would never let go, burrowing into the folds of his blue cotton dressing-gown until his skin was warm against her cheek. The male muskiness of his body filled her senses, and slowly her panic subsided, as other feelings rose inside her.

Dimly she became aware of the storm raging outside. There was no more music from the bar. She touched the collar of Sean's dressing-gown, realising that he must have been in bed when her cries had disturbed him. Resolutely she tried to focus her mind, and untangled herself from his arms.

'What time is it?' she managed to ask.

'About four o'clock.'

'Oh.' She kept her eyes lowered, shy. 'I'm sorry. I didn't mean to wake you.'

'I wasn't asleep.'

Something in the tone of his voice made her look up into his eyes, and what she saw there told her that it wasn't the storm that had kept him awake. She hesitated, unsure—there were so many questions still to be answered. But questions could wait until tomorrow. Fate had given her one last chance to reach him and she wasn't going to throw it away. Heat shimmered between them, and slowly they melted together, their lips meeting in a kiss that stirred the smouldering embers of their earlier encounter.

Kate curled her fingers into the crisp hair at the nape of his neck, reaching up to him yearningly; holding nothing back as he plundered deeply into the sweetest corners of her mouth. He lifted her across his lap, his hands caressing her body through the fine cotton of her pyjamas. And then she felt him brush the fabric aside, felt his long, clever fingers curve possessively over her naked breast. Her tender nipple ripened in respose, and the pleasure washed through her in a warm flood.

Without a word he picked her up, and carried her across the corridor to his own room. The bed was big and comfortable, still warm from his body, and she drew him to her as he laid her down. He was all tenderness, as if to make up for the harsh way he had treated her before, and their bodies communicated as perfectly as they did beneath the water.

He stripped her slowly, savouring every inch of her warm flesh as he uncovered it, and she pulled off his dressing-gown, thrilling to the latent strength of the hard muscles across his back, trailing her fingertips down the cleft of his spine, challenging the exciting danger of a barely restrained male response. If she had only this one night, she wanted it to be a night that would sear her mind for ever. And she would make sure that Sean remembered it too, remembered her amid all the other one-night stands.

Their bodies entwined, exchanging pleasure for pleasure, the touch of flesh against naked flesh inflaming them both. His sensuous tongue swept languorously over the sensitive membranes of her mouth, plumbing the sweetest depths. Her fevered blood coursed through her veins, swirling her into a world of carnal pleasure far beyond her wildest imaginings.

Their mouths broke apart as they dragged air into their lungs in harsh, ragged gasps. His kisses dusted scorching heat over her fluttering eyelids, the delicate shell of her ear, and down over the vulnerable curve of her throat. His hands caressed her ripe, aching breasts, and she moaned softly as with exquisite skill he teased the tender buds of her nipples until they hardened in response. His lips and tongue joined in the game, nibbling and suckling and making her cry out with the intensity of the pleasure.

And then he moved on, over her smooth, downy stomach, her slender thighs, and she quivered beneath his touch, inviting every intimacy, responding wantonly as he led her to unbelievable heights of ecstasy. His eyes and hands and melting kisses savoured every part of her, and in return she explored his strong masculine body, finding the ways to arouse that fierce animal hunger in him.

Their hearts raced in a thundering duet, and Kate was hardly aware that she was crying as he took her, knowing only the sheer joy of being one with him, of soaring free and wild like the hurricane winds through a sky of dark, swirling clouds — to crash and fall at last, spent and exhausted, still tangled in each other's arms.

Afterwards he cradled her gently against his

shoulder, and murmured softly, 'Go to sleep, little Kate.'

Those were the only words that had been spoken since he had carried her into his room. Her heart ached to tell him that she loved him—but so many unanswered questions still lay between them.

This moment was so precious, so perfect, that she didn't want to spoil it. So she feigned sleep, letting her breathing become deep and even, her body heavy. She knew that he was still awake. Outside the storm was raging at the height of its fury, the wind driven rain lashing over the rooftops, and slowly a pale glimmer of dawn crept into the room.

Carefully Sean laid her down on the pillow, and moved silently away from her. She watched him secretly from beneath her lashes as he walked over to the window, and stood gazing out between the slats of the shutters at the grey, stormy sky. He stood there for a long, long time. Her eyes grew heavy, and closed.

She opened them as she heard the sound of the door closing, and sat up quickly, her voice strangled in her throat. He had gone—without a word. His clothes, which had been thrown over a chair, were gone too. She turned her face into the hollow of the pillow where his head had lain, too broken even to cry.

She woke again as the door opened. It was full daylight, and the storm was a little quieter. She started up, hope surging wildly inside her. But it was Maxie, a warm smile curving her generous mouth as she came into the room carrying a breakfast tray. Tears stung Kate's eyes, and she blushed in embarrassment that

Maxie should find her thus in Sean's bed.

Maxie put the tray down on the bedside table, and perched on the edge of the bed. 'He's gone,' she said. It was a statement, not a question. Kate nodded dumbly. 'Don't feel too bad about it,' Maxie said gently. 'He's always like that.'

Kate took a deep, steadying breath. 'Will he come back?' she asked.

Maxie shook her head. 'Not until you've gone.'

'Why?' asked Kate bleakly.

Maxie shrugged her slim shoulders. 'He just doesn't like to let anyone get too close,' she explained.

Kate reached out an urgent hand, and gripped Maxie's wrist. 'Maxie,' she whispered tensely, 'he told me something awful. He told me that ... that he'd killed someone.' Maxie stared down at her blankly. 'It isn't true?'

Maxie shook her head. 'It wasn't Sean,' she said. 'It was ... it was ...'

Her voice faltered, and her face went white. She tried to pull away, but Kate held her in a frozen grip. 'Tell me,' she demanded in a strained voice.

Tears rose to Maxie's eyes, and she sank down on to the edge of the bed again. 'Didn't you know?' Kate shook her head. 'I didn't realise who you were,' Maxie went on. 'It was so long ago—twelve years. I'd all but forgotten it. But the night before you sailed, Sean told me.'

'What happened, Maxie?' pleaded Kate desolately.

Maxie sighed, 'I suppose I have to tell you,' she conceded. 'I wish it didn't have to be me.' She paused, staring down at her feet. Kate waited.

'Like I said, it was twelve years ago,' Maxie began. 'Sean and Dave had met at college—some sort of exchange scheme. They became real good friends. They used to spend nearly all their time on Sean's boat, the old *Barracuda*. There were girls and parties all the time, and they were always going off shark-hunting or diving for sunken treasure.

'Then Sean happened to tell Dave about that old pirate ship, and after that nothing could stop Dave going to find it. So they went off one weekend, and when Dave got back he was so excited . . . He rang all the papers, and the radio stations, and told them he was going to mount an expedition.

'Sean wasn't so keen—he said the wreck was too dangerous. But Dave wouldn't listen to him. He roped in some friends who used to go diving with them sometimes, and badgered Sean until he agreed to take them out again. Anyway, the second day they were there, there was a terrible accident. It was Sean's turn to be top-side crew, and Dave had gone down with the other three . . .'

Kate's eyes widened as the story began to weave a pattern that echoed a memory in her brain. 'They ran out of air!' she put in.

'Yes.' Maxie looked at her searchingly. 'So you did know.'

Kate shook her head. 'Not that it was Sean. No wonder he tried to avoid me when I first arrived, and didn't want to take me out to find the *Belle Étoile*.'

Maxie nodded. 'It brought it all back to him, the inquest and the trial. The way all those people he'd thought were his friends began to doubt him, began to make excuses for staying away. He's never really trusted anyone since then, except the few of us who stood by him. I'm sorry, Kate,' she added gravely, 'I know Dave was your husband, and that I shouldn't speak ill of the dead, but I've never forgiven him for what he did to Sean. I couldn't believe it when I saw him standing up there in the witness box and swearing on oath that it had been Sean's fault.'

'But ... it was the air-tanks. They weren't filled properly. If Sean was top-side crew, it was his responsibility, especially with inexperienced divers who might forget to check for themselves. It was negligence, criminal negligence ...'

Maxie looked at her in surprise. 'Surely you don't believe that?' she demanded sharply.

'I ... but ... then what did happen?' Kate asked, not sure if she wanted to hear the answer.

'Sean said Dave kept them down too long. He said Dave forgot to make allowances for their inexperience, and that they'd used up their air more quickly than he did. He said they probably panicked when their air ran out, and did something wrong, and that's why they drowned.'

'But one of them survived,' Kate argued urgently. 'What did he say happened?'

Maxie's eyes darkened. 'Look, so far as Larry was concerned, Dave had saved his life. Whatever Dave said, Larry agreed with it.'

Kate lay back against the pillows, her mind in shock. 'So what happened at the trial?' she asked. 'Did Sean go to prison?'

'No,' said Maxie. 'The judge said it was one man's

word against another's, and ruled it was insufficient evidence.'

Kate let go her breath in a long sigh. 'But you believe it was Dave's fault, don't you?' she asked.

'Yes, I do.' There was utter conviction in Maxie's voice.

Kate closed her eyes as the tears welled up. 'No,' she protested. 'Dave wouldn't lie like that.'

'Do you think Sean would?' challenged Maxie angrily.

'I don't know. I don't really know him at all.'

'Don't you?' insisted Maxie. 'You've been sailing with him for three weeks, diving with him, sleeping with him. I'd have thought you'd know him pretty well by now.'

Kate opened her eyes and stared at her. 'Where is he, Maxie?' she demanded urgently.

Maxie evaded her gaze. 'I don't know,' she demurred.

'He's down at the *Barracuda*, isn't he?' Kate persisted, reaching for her pyjamas. 'I'm going to find him, and ask him myself. I don't care if he doesn't want to see me. I've got to know the truth.'

Maxie sighed. 'Okay, yes. He's down at the *Barracuda*,' she admitted. 'Only don't tell him I told you where to find him. How's your ankle?' she added sympathetically as Kate set her foot gingerly on the floor.

'It'll get me as far as the harbour,' vowed Kate grimly.

Maxie gave her a wry grin. 'You know, I really ought to be scratching your eyes out,' she mused. 'But I think I'll wish you luck instead.'

As Kate emerged from the shelter of the buildings the wind hit her full force, almost bowling her over. She struggled along the quayside, limping painfully, drenched to the skin. The storm-tossed boats battered against each other on an angry grey sea. Some had been badly damaged, but the *Barracuda* was well built and expertly tied up.

The deck was pitching violently, and Kate regretted her brief glance down into the boiling water beneath the stern. Taking a deep breath, she paced the steep rise and fall of the boat, and then jumped, grabbing the rail as she landed. She let go her breath in a sigh of relief, but the battle was only half won. She dragged herself round the aft-deck until she reached the main door, and quickly pressed out the combination of the lock.

The force of the wind made it difficult to slide the door open, and she half-fell down the steps, and turned to wrestle the door shut. As the deafening howl of the wind was muffled by the closing of the door she heard a noise behind her, and turned. Sean was standing in the doorway to the for'ard cabins. He hadn't shaved, and his jaw was rough with stubble. In his fist he was clutching a half-empty bottle of whisky, and his blue eyes glittered with cold hostility.

'What the hell are you doing here?' he growled.

'I wanted to see you,' said Kate, breathless from her fight against the wind.

'Well, I don't want to see you. The one-night stand's

over. Thank you for being a real good lay. Now get out of here.'

'You're drunk,' she accused, stung by his cruel words, though she had expected no better.

He gave a hollow laugh. 'Not nearly as drunk as I'm going to be,' he vowed grimly. He turned his back on her, and vanished down the steps to his cabin.

'Sean, I just want to talk to you,' she pleaded, following him.

He turned and confronted her again, his hard mouth curved into an ugly sneer. 'What do you want, Mrs Taylor?' he demanded bitterly. 'Do you want me to tell you that you were different from all the others? That I was in love with you? Well, do you?'

She stared up at him bleakly, tears stinging her eyes. 'Sean, please . . .'

'Because it's true,' he grated. 'Go on, laugh. It's a joke—a big, sick joke.' He turned away from her again, and threw himself down on the big oval bed, taking a deep swig from the whisky bottle.

She moved uncertainly towards him.

'I knew I was in trouble from the first moment I saw you,' he went on bitterly. 'That first night in the Runner—remember that? You walked down those steps, and you looked like a pearl —a beautiful pearl among all that dross. I wanted you right then, even though I guessed at once who you were.'

Cautiously Kate sat down on the edge of the bunk, her eyes never leaving his.

'You've been driving me crazy ever since.' He cast a disgusted glance at the whisky bottle. 'Look at me, trying to drown my sorrows in drink.' He put the bottle down on the floor, and lifted his hands to grip her shoulders. 'I should never have let you talk me into taking you out to look for that damn wreck. I should have stuck with my first instinct, and stayed well away from you.

'But I couldn't. You got under my skin until I couldn't leave you alone. Last weekend—I decided to get away from you for a few days, to try to recover my sanity. Then first I let myself stay and have dinner with you, then I spent the whole time thinking about you, until I had to come back and fetch you.

'Then, on the beach, just for a moment, it seemed as though it was all going to come right after all. But it was too much to hope for, wasn't it, little Kate?' Absently he twirled a finger round one curl of her hair. 'The past was too strong for us.'

The sorrow in his voice twisted her heart. 'Why wouldn't you tell me what happened between you and Dave?' she whispered urgently.

He closed his eyes. 'Why did you have to come looking for me?' he groaned. 'Why couldn't you have gone back to England, and left me with the memory of last night?'

She gripped the front of his shirt in tight little fists. 'I'm not going anywhere until you tell me the truth,' she insisted fiercely.

He opened his eyes again, and gazed up into hers as if trying to see right into her soul. 'The truth?' he repeated reluctantly.

'Please, Sean,' she begged. 'Otherwise I'll never be sure.'

'You're not sure now?'

She shook her head. 'Not any more. I only knew Dave's version—he didn't even tell me himself, I heard it from someone else. I had no idea it was you, until Maxie told me.'

He was watching her warily. 'So now you know both versions,' he said, his voice so guarded that there was no expression in it at all. 'Which one are you going to believe?'

'Is yours the truth?' she asked tensely.

'Yes.'

She took a long, steadying breath. Suddenly everything was falling into place. She nodded slowly. 'Then I believe you.' She stood up, and moved across to look out of the port-hole. The hurricane was passing now. Soon everybody would begin picking up the pieces, the sun would come out, and life in the islands would return to its usual tranquillity.

'It would have been so like Dave to forget the time,' she mused sadly. 'He used to get so involved . . . I don't think he even meant to lie. He just wouldn't have been able to face up to what he'd done. He probably completely convinced himself that it was your fault.'

'You're still in love with him,' said Sean, his voice rough with pain.

'Yes. I think I always will be, in one little corner of my heart.' She turned back to face Sean. 'But I think I know him better now—and myself.' She smiled wryly. 'You were right, you know. I did have a sort of adolescent crush on him. I was a little more than an adolescent when I met him—I'd been a bit sheltered by my parents, I suppose. He seemed like, oh, some hero out of a romantic novel. Maybe it could have grown into something more adult—I'll never know.'

'What will you do now?' he asked gently. A soft blush rose to her cheeks, and her silken lashes swept down. 'Don't go back to England,' he urged. 'Stay here with me. I can offer you endless sunshine, and the most beautiful coral reefs in the world. And I love you,' he added, a trace of uncertainty in his voice, as if he was a little unsure that that would count.

A tiny glow of happiness was growing in Kate's heart. 'On one condition,' she teased. He lifted an enquiring eyebrow. 'That we don't have to live over the shop.'

His rich laughter filled the room. 'You mean the Runner? No, we don't have to live there if we don't want to. Maxie could do with more space anyway when her kids are home from school. We can live where you like.'

She smiled happily. 'Then it's a deal,' she agreed.

He held out his hand, and she took it, and let him draw her over to sit beside him. 'Just tell me one thing, little Kate,' he asked gruffly. 'Am I still second best?'

She shook her head, smiling down into his eyes. 'No,' she whispered, reaching out one trembling hand to stroke his rough cheek. 'I love you, Sean.'

He wrapped his arms around her, and bundled her down on to the bunk beside him. The whisky fumes on his breath almost made her faint. 'Phew! You *are* drunk!' she protested.

'I know,' he mumbled, drawing back. 'I'm sorry. Are you going to make me sober up before I can ask you to marry me?'

Kate reached up and drew him down to her again,

knowing that she had a better way than mere words to give him her answer.

Harlequin Presents

Coming Next Month

Available in January wherever paperback books are sold, or through Harlequin Reader Service:

In the U.S.
901 Fuhrmann Blvd.
P.O. Box 1397
Buffalo, N.Y. 14240-1397

In Canada
P.O. Box 603
Fort Erie, Ontario
L2A 5X3

"GIVE YOUR HEART TO HARLEQUIN" SWEEPSTAKES
OFFICIAL RULES

NO PURCHASE NECESSARY TO ENTER OR RECEIVE A PRIZE

1. To enter and join the Preview Service, scratch off the concealment device on all game tickets. This will reveal the values for each Sweepstakes entry number, the number of free books you will receive, and your free bonus gift as part of our Preview Service. If you do not wish to take advantage of our Preview Service, only scratch off the concealment device on game tickets 1-3. To enter, return your entire sheet of tickets.

2. Either way your Sweepstakes numbers will be compared against the list of winning numbers generated at random by computer. In the event that all prizes are not claimed, random drawings will be held from all entries received from all presentations to award all unclaimed prizes. All cash prizes are payable in U.S. funds. This is in addition to any free, surprise or mystery gifts that might be offered. Versions of this Sweepstakes with different prizes may appear in other mailings or at retail outlets by Torstar Ltd. and its affiliates. This presentation offers the following prizes:

(1)	*Grand Prize	$1,000,000 Annuity
(1)	First Prize	$25,000
(2)	Second Prize	$10,000
(5)	Third Prize	$5,000
(10)	Fourth Prize	$1,000
(2,000)	Fifth Prize	$10

   . . . *This presentation contains a Grand Prize offering of a $1,000,000 annuity. Winner may elect to receive $25,000 a year for life up to $1,000,000 or $250,000 in one cash payment. Winners selected will receive the prizes offered in the Sweepstakes promotion they receive.

   Entrants may cancel Preview Service at any time without cost or obligation (see details in the center insert card).

3. This promotion is being conducted under the supervision of Marden-Kane, an independent judging organization. By entering the Sweepstakes, each entrant accepts and agrees to be bound by these rules and the decisions of the judges which shall be final and binding. Odds of winning in the random drawing are dependent upon the total number of entries received. Taxes, if any, are the sole responsibility of the winners. Prizes are non-transferable. All entries must be received by March 31, 1988. The drawing will take place on April 30, 1988 at the offices of Marden-Kane, Lake Success, New York.

4. This offer is open to residents of the U.S., Great Britain and Canada, 18 years or older except employees of Torstar Ltd., its affiliates, subsidiaries, Marden-Kane and all other agencies and persons connected with conducting this Sweepstakes. All Federal, State and local laws apply. Void wherever prohibited or restricted by law.

5. Winners will be notified by mail and may be required to execute an affidavit of eligibility and release which must be returned within 14 days after notification. Canadian winners will be required to answer a skill testing question. Winners consent to the use of their name, photograph and/or likeness for advertising and publicity in conjunction with this and similar promotions without additional compensation. One prize per family or household.

6. For a list of our most current prize winners, send a stamped, self-addressed envelope to: WINNERS LIST c/o MARDEN-KANE, P.O. BOX 701, SAYREVILLE, N.J. 08872.

Six exciting series for you every month... from Harlequin

Harlequin Romance·
The series that started it all

Tender, captivating and heartwarming...
love stories that sweep you off to faraway places
and delight you with the magic of love.

◆

Harlequin Presents·
Powerful contemporary love stories...as individual as the women who read them

The No. 1 romance series...
exciting love stories for you, the woman of today...
a rare blend of passion and dramatic realism.

◆

Harlequin Superromance®
It's more than romance...
it's Harlequin Superromance

A sophisticated, contemporary romance-fiction
series, providing you with a longer,
more involving read...a richer mix of complex plots,
realism and adventure.

Harlequin
American Romance™
Harlequin celebrates the American woman...

...by offering you romance stories written about American women, by American women for American women. This series offers you contemporary romances uniquely North American in flavor and appeal.

◆

Harlequin Temptation
Passionate stories for today's woman

An exciting series of sensual, mature stories of love...dilemmas, choices, resolutions... all contemporary issues dealt with in a true-to-life fashion by some of your favorite authors.

◆

Harlequin Intrigue
Because romance can be quite an adventure

Harlequin Intrigue, an innovative series that blends the romance you expect... with the unexpected. Each story has an added element of intrigue that provides a new twist to the Harlequin tradition of romance excellence.

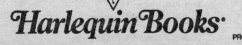

Harlequin Books·

PROD-A-2